REALITY TELEVISION
GUILTY PLEASURE OR POSITIVE INFLUENCE?

By Tyler Stevenson

Portions of this book originally appeared in *Reality TV* by Shannon Kelly.

LUCENT
P R E S S

Published in 2020 by
Lucent Press, an Imprint of Greenhaven Publishing, LLC
353 3rd Avenue
Suite 255
New York, NY 10010

Designer: Deanna Paternostro
Editor: Jennifer Lombardo

Cataloging-in-Publication Data

Names: Stevenson, Tyler.
Title: Reality television: guilty pleasure or positive influence? / Tyler Stevenson.
Description: New York : Lucent Press, 2020. | Series: Hot topics | Includes glossary and index.
Identifiers: ISBN 9781534567634 (pbk.) | ISBN 9781534567009 (library bound) | ISBN 9781534567641 (ebook)
Subjects: LCSH: Reality television programs–Social aspects–Juvenile literature. | Reality television programs–Psychological aspects–Juvenile literature. | Reality television programs–Moral and ethical aspects–Juvenile literature.
Classification: LCC PN1992.8.R43 S748 2020 | DDC 791.456–dc23

Printed in the United States of America

CPSIA compliance information: Batch #BS19KL: For further information contact Greenhaven Publishing LLC, New York, New York at 1-844-317-7404.

Please visit our website, www.greenhavenpublishing.com. For a free color catalog of all our high-quality books, call toll free 1-844-317-7404 or fax 1-844-317-7405.

CONTENTS

FOREWORD 4

INTRODUCTION 6
A Dominant Force in Television

CHAPTER 1 11
Defining Reality Television

CHAPTER 2 31
Why Is Reality Television Popular?

CHAPTER 3 43
Start Getting "Real"

CHAPTER 4 56
Positives and Negatives

CHAPTER 5 74
Reality Television in the Future

NOTES 86

DISCUSSION QUESTIONS 93

ORGANIZATIONS TO CONTACT 95

FOR MORE INFORMATION 96

INDEX 98

PICTURE CREDITS 103

ABOUT THE AUTHOR 104

Adolescence is a time when many people begin to take notice of the world around them. News channels, blogs, and talk radio shows are constantly promoting one view or another; very few are unbiased. Young people also hear conflicting information from parents, friends, teachers, and acquaintances. Often, they will hear only one side of an issue or be given flawed information. People who are trying to support a particular viewpoint may cite inaccurate facts and statistics on their blogs, and news programs present many conflicting views of important issues in our society. In a world where it seems everyone has a platform to share their thoughts, it can be difficult to find unbiased, accurate information about important issues.

It is not only facts that are important. In blog posts, in comments on online videos, and on talk shows, people will share opinions that are not necessarily true or false, but can still have a strong impact. For example, many young people struggle with their body image. Seeing or hearing negative comments about particular body types online can have a huge effect on the way someone views himself or herself and may lead to depression and anxiety. Although it is important not to keep information hidden from young people under the guise of protecting them, it is equally important to offer encouragement on issues that affect their mental health.

The titles in the Hot Topics series provide readers with different viewpoints on important issues in today's society. Many of these issues, such as gang violence and gun control laws, are of immediate concern to young people. This series aims to give readers factual context on these crucial topics in a way that lets them form their own opinions. The facts presented throughout also serve to empower readers to help themselves or support people they know who are struggling with many of the challenges adolescents face today. Although negative viewpoints are not ignored or downplayed, this series allows young people to see that the challenges they face are not insurmountable. As increasing numbers of young adults join political debates, especially regarding gun violence, learning the facts as well as the views of others will help them decide where they stand—and understand what they are fighting for.

Quotes encompassing all viewpoints are presented and cited so readers can trace them back to their original source, verifying for themselves whether the information comes from a reputable place. Additional books and websites are listed, giving readers a starting point from which to continue their own research. Chapter questions encourage discussion, allowing young people to hear and understand their classmates' points of view as they further solidify their own. Full-color photographs and enlightening charts provide a deeper understanding of the topics at hand. All of these features augment the informative text, helping young people understand the world they live in and formulate their own opinions concerning the best way they can improve it.

A Dominant Force in Television

When people think of reality television, what often comes to mind is guilty pleasure shows about wealthy socialites behaving terribly, eccentric people on wild vacations, and fame-hungry people desperately competing for the attention and love of someone that they just met. While the *Real Housewives* franchise, *Jersey Shore*, and *The Bachelor* certainly qualify as notable examples of this genre of television, there are countless other examples that many people may not call to mind as quickly. Reality TV programs can be straightforward game shows such as *Jeopardy!* and *The Price is Right*; programs that are a combination of documentary and competition, such as *The Voice* and *The Amazing Race*; or shows that simply follow people doing the jobs they do every day, such as *Trauma: Life in the ER* and *Million Dollar Listing*.

Today, it may feel as though every single channel is broadcasting reality programs for most of the day. Even the Weather Channel has reality TV offerings such as *Storm Stories* and *Highway Thru Hell*. The explosion of reality TV continues as more and more programs following various minor celebrities and their families are announced annually.

A quick glance at the television listings for any day of the week reveals dozens of reality shows that deal with a variety of topics. According to the *New York Times*,

> The genre started as a mix of the moderately silly and the formulaic: survivalist competitions for people willing to eat insects; on-the-job series that followed police officers or ambulance crews. But as the phenomenon expanded … things grew both weirder

and more ordinary. On the weird end of the spectrum there were suddenly shows about pathological hoarders and people eaten by their own pets. But there were also shows about people merely doing the everyday: driving a big-rig truck for a living; running a beauty salon.[1]

Reality television has continued to explode as a genre over the past several years. In 2016, Courteney Monroe, the CEO of National Geographic Global Networks, reported that about 750 reality TV shows—350 of which were brand new series— had aired the previous year on cable channels during prime time (from 8 p.m. to 11 p.m. on weeknights). This was 83 percent more than the number of scripted shows that aired the same year on prime time cable. However, since not all reality shows air on prime time cable, the actual number is likely much higher.

People commonly joke that MTV no longer has much to do with music because of how many reality shows it airs.

These numbers indicate that reality TV has remained immensely popular since the debut arguably the most influential reality show of all: MTV's 1992 pioneer, *The Real World*. While the popularity of reality television has decreased since its peak in the 2007 to 2008 TV season, tens of millions of people are still consistently watching programs such as *The Voice*, *Dancing with the Stars*, and *Survivor* as of 2019. *Survivor*, in particular, has had remarkable staying power, considering that it kicked off the modern-day boom in reality programming. While *The Real World* is rightfully seen as a massively influential trailblazer in the world of reality TV, it aired on a cable channel that not everyone wanted—or could afford—to watch. In contrast, *Survivor* aired on a major broadcast network and found a huge audience immediately. Since its premiere in 2000, it has spun off into dozens of different versions in other countries and led to shows with a similar concept, such as *The Amazing Race*.

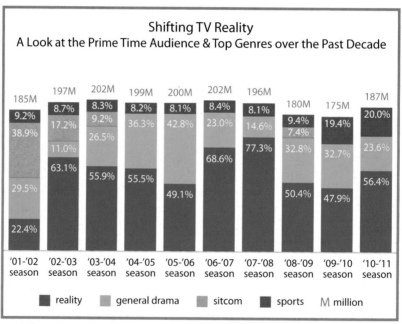

While reality TV has declined in popularity since 2008, it still makes up a large amount of TV programming, as this information from Nielsen—a company that measures TV ratings—shows.

Undeniably Popular

Reality TV is undeniably popular with a large number of viewers. However, people who see it as inferior to scripted programming often disregard it as immoral or worthless. As journalist and TV critic James Poniewozik wrote in *TIME* magazine, "It is the one mass-entertainment category that thrives because of its audience's contempt for it. It makes us feel tawdry, dirty, cheap—if it didn't, we probably wouldn't bother tuning in."[2] While some people agree with him, others believe this is an unfair statement based on a narrow definition of what, exactly, is considered reality television. These reality TV supporters point out that for every show such as *The Real Housewives of Orange County*, depicting wealthy white women throwing drinks in each other's faces, there is a show rewarding the creativity and talent of its contestants, such as *Project Runway*. Other reality programs show the difficulties people with disabilities face in modern society. These include shows such as *Little People, Big World*, which follows a family in which the parents and one of their children have dwarfism, or **Born This Way**, which follows the lives of several people who were born with Down syndrome. People may have a difficult time finding value in a program such as *Joe Millionaire*, in which a network encouraged women to compete with each other for the affections of a fake millionaire. However, it is harder to argue that there is nothing positive to be taken from a program such as *RuPaul's Drag Race*, which celebrates creativity and differences among people, or *Alaska State Troopers*, which shows the difficulties law enforcement agents can face, especially in harsh, unforgiving environments.

The debate over whether or not reality TV is worthwhile will likely continue for the foreseeable future, but regardless of whether a conclusion is reached, the fact remains that the pop culture landscape is filled with reality TV figures. People love to watch people from entertainment news shows such as *TMZ on TV* stopping personalities from these programs on the street and asking them questions about their lives and their opinions on certain issues. Reality TV stars have become so influential that Kim Kardashian West has met with President Donald Trump—a former reality television star himself—in the Oval Office to discuss issues such as prison reform. Even members of Congress can have a difficult time scheduling meetings with the president, which shows how wildly influential reality TV has become. This type of fame and respect is one reason why people want to be on a reality show, but it is not the only one: There

Shown here are Kim Kardashian West and her family at the 2018 March for Our Lives. Some people are happy that reality stars take an interest in issues such as gun control, while others believe they have no business getting involved in politics.

is huge money to be made as well. The Kardashian family, who managed to turn one TV show about their family into a wide-reaching, multimedia empire, is worth hundreds of millions of dollars. As of early 2019, the top earner in the family is Kylie Jenner. By the age of 21, she was nearly a billionaire.

Reality TV may not be the dominating force it was at its peak, but it is still a considerable part of the TV landscape. When ratings for some of TV's biggest reality hits began to decline around 2010, many people predicted that the genre was on its way out, but that has clearly not come to pass. As Poniewozik stated, "Reality TV ... is here to stay, in that it is simply now another genre of TV, like sitcoms or dramas, but like those other genres, it will have boom times and lean times."[3] In the future, people can expect reality television to remain a huge part of the TV landscape and expect the stars of these programs to have an outsized influence on pop culture.

CHAPTER 1

Defining Reality Television

What types of programs can be considered reality TV? Landing on a standard definition has proven difficult. For example, a game show such as *The Price Is Right* involves real people, but most people would not immediately think of a game show if asked to name an example of a reality show. Similarly, few people would name a daytime courtroom show such as *Judge Judy* or a talk show such as *The View*, even though, again, they involve real people and real situations. Therefore, it seems that while most people would know a reality TV show if they saw one, they would also have difficulty describing what one is. Even experts have trouble with this. Media and communications scholar Kevin Glynn described reality television as "a genre (or more accurately a collection of genres) that is not susceptible to easy definition ... because of both its internal diversity and its many overlaps with other sets of television genres."[4]

Robin Nabi, a Department of Communications professor at the University of California, Santa Barbara, and a noted media scholar, wrote an article in 2003 with colleagues Erica Biely, Sara Morgan, and Carmen Stitt in which they defined reality television as programs that "film real people as they live out events (contrived [purposely set up] or otherwise) in their lives, as these events occur."[5] They further narrowed this definition by saying a program in question must meet certain standards. It must involve people being themselves rather than actors playing characters, the participants must be filmed at least in part in their living or working environment rather than on a production set, the program must not be scripted, the events shown on the program must be placed in a narrative context (meaning they must tell some kind of story that unfolds as the viewers watch), and the show must be produced for the main purpose of viewer entertainment.

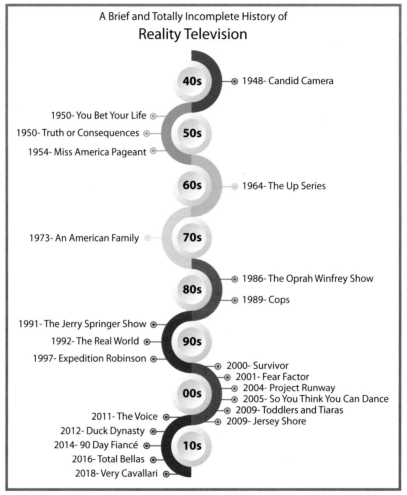

Reality shows have been around nearly as long as TV broadcasting itself, although the topics of these shows have changed much over the years.

Nabi and her colleagues' definition seems reasonably clear when applied to shows such as *Big Brother*, in which strangers are placed in a house together and monitored constantly by cameras, or to programs that involve live performances, such as *The Voice*. It also clearly disqualifies game shows and talk shows because they do not have a narrative context and courtroom shows because the participants are not being filmed in their normal environment. It requires a little more thought, however, to apply that definition to shows such as Syfy's *Destination Truth*, in which a team of adventurers travels the globe in search of mythological creatures and urban legends. According to Nabi, a show being "unscripted" rather than "real" may be the most important identifying feature of the genre. Keeping that in mind, then, *Destination Truth* would be considered a reality show—and so would an unscripted courtroom drama such as *Judge Judy*. Confusingly, though, many reality shows do sometimes create scripted scenarios or conversations for their participants, so it may be more accurate to talk about whether a show is advertised as being unscripted rather than whether it actually is.

Different Kinds of Reality Programs

People who write about TV do not always agree on what types of shows should be included under the reality TV umbrella. One source may list 14 subgroups, while another may list only 10. One may consider sporting events and talk shows to be reality programming; another may not. Writer and former television producer Michael Essany, in his 2008 book *Reality Check: The Business and Art of Producing Reality TV*, lists 12 subgroups: documentary reality, celebrity reality, competition reality, personal improvement and makeover reality, renovation and design reality, professional reality, forced environment reality, romance reality, aspiration reality, fear-based reality, sports reality, and undercover reality.

Documentary-style reality programs are those that take a "fly-on-the-wall" approach, following events objectively as they occur, with—in theory—little involvement by the production team. The groundbreaking 1973 documentary series *An American Family* was an example of this style, as well as recent shows such as *Catfish: The TV Show*, *Hoarders*, *True Life*, and *Teen Mom*.

Celebrity reality shows focus on a well-known personality (though rarely an actual A-list star). While many of these shows feature celebrities filmed living their day-to-day lives in a fairly ordinary manner, such as *Keeping Up with the Kardashians*, others situate celebrities in fake environments, such as on *The Surreal Life*, in which a group of celebrities lives together in a mansion while their interactions are filmed and broadcast.

Competition reality shows include talent-search programs such as *The Voice* and *So You Think You Can Dance*, as well as reality game shows such as *Survivor*. In some cases, the audience can affect the outcome of the competition by voting for a particular contestant on the show. In others, such as *The Amazing Race*, it is the contestants' own hard work and dedication—or lack thereof—that determine how long they remain in the game.

Personal improvement and makeover reality shows are those in which a person's appearance is supposedly changed for the better. These changes can be small, such as simply gaining a new wardrobe or hairstyle through *What Not to Wear* or the recently rebooted *Queer Eye*. Other times, they involve changing a person's body, as in the weight-loss competition *Revenge Body with Khloe Kardashian* or the former Fox show *The Swan*, which offered plastic surgery to those who considered

The cast of Queer Eye *(shown here) has become beloved by millions of viewers.*

themselves unattractive. The goals of renovation and design reality programs are similar, but for living spaces rather than people. Examples include *Extreme Makeover: Home Edition* and *The Property Brothers*. In an interesting twist, *Extreme Makeover: Home Edition* is a spin-off of a makeover show that was simply called *Extreme Makeover*, which, like *The Swan*, featured individuals receiving very drastic makeovers, often including plastic surgery.

Essany divides professional reality programs into two categories: those that focus on people performing their jobs, such as *The First 48* or *Ice Road Truckers*, and those that follow people attempting to achieve success in a certain career, such as *America's Next Top Model*. Forced environment reality shows are those that take strangers and confine them together in a fake environment that the producers can change or influence. *Big Brother* and *The Real World* fall into this category. These programs are not necessarily scripted, but the participants are often purposely put in uncomfortable situations that are meant to generate a specific reaction or maximize drama.

PERSONALITY VERSUS SKILL

"The sad part of reality television is its exploitive nature. Few, if any, participants are famous because of hard work, talent or skill. They achieve reality stardom because they are willing to expose and exploit a portion of their private lives."

–Kelly Boggs, online columnist

Kelly Boggs, "Reality TV: Why Do People Watch?, *Baptist Press*, April 8, 2011. www.bpnews.net/BPFirstPerson.asp?ID=35022.

Romance reality shows such as *The Bachelor* and *The Bachelorette* attempt to make love connections for or between cast members. Aspiration programs are similar to competition or professional programs, but they focus more on the journey toward success and often do not crown an actual winner. This type of show is less common, but one of the best-known examples is MTV's *Made*, which aired from 2003 to 2014. This show followed teens as they worked to achieve certain dreams, such as becoming professional singers or athletes. More recently, *My 600-lb Life* follows people who weigh 600 pounds or more as they attempt to lose weight, chronicling their emotional and physical struggles and successes.

Fear-based reality shows include *Fear Factor*, which involved placing contestants in situations that required them to do things they found scary or disgusting. Arguably, shows such as *Ghost Hunters*, *Ghost Adventures*, and *Most Haunted* also fall into this category. Sports reality shows are those that feature competitions between athletes. Examples include *American Ninja Warrior* (obstacle course), *Ultimate Fighter* (mixed martial arts) and *The Big Break* (golfing). The final category, undercover reality shows, can take two different forms. One type includes shows such as *Impractical Jokers*, which involve playing pranks on people or filming them in unusual situations. They are considered undercover shows because the people do not know they are being filmed until the prank is over. In the other type, "undercover" refers more to the subject of the show than the camera. For example, *Undercover Boss* involves the head of a major company putting on a disguise and working at some of their locations. The other workers do not know the real identity of their boss, but they know they are being filmed; they are generally told that a documentary is being made.

Essany admits there are shows that do not fit easily into any of the subgroups he names. Additionally, on many occasions, reality programs cross multiple genres. The hugely popular *Dancing with the Stars* is both a celebrity reality program and a competition program. *Rock of Love with Bret Michaels* was a celebrity/romance program, following the long-haired front man of the 1980s rock band Poison and the women competing for his affections. There are even renovation reality programs featuring celebrities flipping houses, such as *The Vanilla Ice Project* and *A Very Brady Renovation*, in which the cast of the 1970s sitcom *The Brady Bunch* reunited in 2019 to renovate the house whose exterior appeared on the show. It is almost impossible to turn on the television and not find a program following a minor

Some reality shows can fit into multiple genres. Dancing with the Stars is both a celebrity reality program and a competition reality program.

celebrity doing a task or job they did not originally become famous for. This cross typing is a major reason that scholars find it difficult to agree on an "official" list of reality television subgroups.

Reality TV: The Beginning

The earliest reality television shows were relatively simple and easy to place into categories. Although many people associate reality programming with the boom of the 2000s, MTV's *The Real World* in the 1990s is often considered to be the first real example of the genre. However, this is only partially true. It is technically the first example of reality TV as it is known today, but the genre was born much earlier than that. The first game show to be televised in the United States, *Uncle Jim's Question Bee,* debuted in July 1941, more than 50 years prior to the launch of *The Real World.* Apart from game shows, the first show generally considered to be a reality program was NBC's undercover show *Candid Camera,* in which pranks were pulled on unsuspecting participants while hidden cameras recorded their reactions. It first hit the television airwaves in 1948.

The next major milestone in reality television happened in 1973 with the premiere of the groundbreaking *An American Family* on PBS. The 12-episode documentary series followed the

A Groundbreaking Series

Candid Camera is considered by many media scholars to be the first comedy reality television show. It began as a radio program called *The Candid Microphone* in 1947 and then moved to ABC's television network in 1948. *Candid Camera* was created by Allen Funt, a New Yorker who attended the Pratt Institute and Cornell and Columbia Universities before landing a job at an advertising agency. The basic idea of the show was to put unsuspecting people in awkward or unusual situations and secretly record their reactions. In one example of a classic stunt, the show rigged a speaker inside a public mailbox, and when a man tried to mail a letter, the box began "talking" to him. When the man attempted to tell a passing policeman about the talking mailbox, it refused to speak. When the prank had run its course, the victim was clued in to what was happening by the show's famous tag line: "Smile! You're on *Candid Camera!*"

The show ran on and off for more than 60 years, changing networks several times. Allen Funt himself hosted the earlier seasons of the show, with his son Peter joining him and eventually taking over as host in the later seasons. Allen Funt became so well-known to the general public that in 1969, when a Miami-bound plane he and his camera crew were on was hijacked, all the other passengers believed it was a *Candid Camera* stunt—despite Funt's attempts to convince them otherwise—until the plane landed in Cuba instead of Miami. The most recent version of the show ran in 2014 for 10 episodes on the TV Land cable channel. Peter Funt and Mayim Bialik, who is best known for her role as Amy Farrah Fowler on *The Big Bang Theory*, cohosted it.

Loud family over the course of seven months. The Louds were an upper-middle-class family consisting of parents Bill and Pat Loud and their five children: Lance, Delilah, Grant, Kevin, and Michele. People who tuned in to the show were surprised to find themselves watching the dissolution of a marriage, as Pat and Bill's relationship worsened in front of the cameras. The stated goal of following the Louds' lives was to show how an "average" family responded to the daily concerns facing all families at the time. However, many believe producer Craig Gilbert's motive was to draw attention to the greater collapse of traditional American order by showing the downfall of a "typical" American family. When the series began airing, the Louds were strongly criticized by the public and the press, and many of the unkind words were directed at the oldest son, Lance, who was openly gay at a time when few people felt comfortable admitting their sexuality. Lance Loud is often credited as being the first openly gay person to be a regular fixture on television, and he later became an icon in the gay community. In 2011, HBO premiered a scripted film called *Cinema Verite*, based on the production of *An American Family*.

Shown here is a 1990 photo of Pat and Lance Loud. As a result of An American Family, *Lance became one of the first nationally recognizable gay icons.*

Two more important shows premiered after *An American Family* ended. *Real People*, from 1979, featured interviews with people who had unique jobs or hobbies, and 1980's *That's Incredible!* highlighted people performing unusual and often dangerous stunts. In the late 1980s, reality TV began to tackle more serious topics, such as crime and medical emergencies, in programs such as *Unsolved Mysteries* (1987), *America's Most Wanted* (1988), and *Rescue 911* (1989). The year 1989 also saw the debut of *Cops*, one of the longest-running reality TV programs, which entered its 31st season in 2018. The iconic show follows real-life police officers as they go on patrols and arrest suspects.

The Real World, which is generally considered to be the modern-day pioneer of reality TV, debuted on MTV in 1992. The show featured a group of young strangers of different genders, races, religions, backgrounds, and sexual orientations who were selected by the producers to live together in a house (The first season took place in New York, but the city varied each season.) while their interpersonal relationships were recorded and broadcast. Frequently, the housemates were also sent on vacations together or given a group project to complete, such as starting a business, as a way to highlight their interactions and increase public interest.

While it took some time to familiarize MTV's target audience with the show, it caught on and began drawing 1 million viewers per episode, ushering in a new era of reality TV. As Matthew Gilbert of the *Boston Globe* put it, "*The Real World* was the first time TV told viewers in earnest that ordinary lives could be transformed into lively entertainment programming. Real people had been on game shows, talent contests, and documentaries, but the ... idea that they could star as dramatic or comic figures with their own plot arcs was new."[6]

Early seasons of *The Real World* were praised by the media for their willingness to openly explore topics such as prejudice, sexuality, abortion, addiction, and political and religious differences. Famously, the third season, which was set in San Francisco, California, featured cast member Pedro Zamora, an openly gay AIDS activist, and his commitment ceremony with his partner,

Sean Sasser. This was the first on-screen example of such a ceremony for a same-sex couple.

The first cast of The Real World *is shown here at an MTV event in 1992. This groundbreaking show featured people from different walks of life that were often not shown on television at that time.*

The third season has been credited with turning the show from a relatively popular curiosity to a true hit for MTV. Later seasons, however, have been criticized as simply a showcase for bad behavior, drinking, fighting, and casual sex. Reality TV critic Andy Denhart believes that bad behavior has always been part of the show but that the motivations for that behavior have changed. In 2011, he wrote, "What once was the result of relationships between people with different backgrounds has become behavior from people who know they will get more attention and become more famous the more outrageously they act."[7] The show ran for 32 seasons, and although it was put on hold in 2017, MTV announced plans in 2018 to revive the show and potentially feature it on a streaming platform such as Netflix. *The Real World* has seen multiple popular spinoffs over the years as well—notably *Road Rules*, a competition show that ran for 14 seasons, and *The Challenge*, another competition show

The Enduring Legacy of Pedro Zamora

Pedro Zamora, a Cuban American, was one of the first openly gay men to appear in a television series. He was also an AIDS educator who was himself living with the disease. AIDS, or acquired immunodeficiency syndrome, is a deadly sexually transmitted disease that struck the gay community especially hard in the 1980s and 1990s. Probably the best-known person to ever appear on *The Real World*, Zamora opened the eyes of many MTV viewers to the risks of AIDS as he taught his fellow house members about the illness. These viewers also saw a loving, dedicated gay relationship between Zamora and his boyfriend, Sean Sasser, which was highlighted with an emotional commitment ceremony performed in front of the show's cameras.

President Bill Clinton praised Zamora for his work as an AIDS activist and called the young man to offer support when Zamora was hospitalized after the show finished filming. Zamora died at the age of 22 on November 11, 1994—the day after the last episode of *The Real World: San Francisco* aired. He is still mourned by many fans of the show and those who were influenced by his life.

President Clinton introduced the premiere of *Pedro*, a 2009 movie about Zamora's life, with the words, "To this day, Pedro Zamora remains an extraordinary example of what a huge impact one young person can make in our world."[1]

1. Quoted in Hal Boedecker, "Reality Star's Riveting Message Still Resonates in Film," *Orlando Sentinel*, April 1, 2009. articles.orlandosentinel.com/2009-04-01/news/pedro01_1_pedro-zamora-alex-loynaz-real-world.

that featured former members of *The Real World* and *Road Rules* pitted against each other.

In 1999, the game show *Who Wants to Be a Millionaire?* was adapted from the British version and hit the American airwaves. Viewers were excited by the show because ordinary people—not just those with genius IQ levels—could qualify as contestants simply by calling a number and answering a few questions. In its first season, *Millionaire* was so popular that ABC aired it five times per week. The show had close to 30 million viewers per episode and actually changed the pattern of phone traffic in the United States. According to Mark Andrejevic in his book *Reality TV: The Work of Being Watched*, "By early 2000, the telephone company noted that the standard lull in telephone activity in the evening (post-work) hours was interrupted by a jagged peak at 10 p.m. (Eastern time), representing the thousands of phone calls made to the *Who Wants to Be a Millionaire* hotline at the end of the show."[8] The show's ratings began to decline steadily after its second season, however, and its prime time version was canceled in 2002. In its place, a daily syndicated (broadcast on multiple stations) version was launched and has aired consistently in the United States ever since. The program has also expanded to multiple other countries, including Australia, Russia, India, and the Philippines.

"DISCOMFORT TV"

"Reality TV—call it 'discomfort TV'—lives to rattle viewers' cages. It provokes. It offends. But at least it's trying to do something besides help you get to sleep."

—James Poniewozik, journalist and TV critic

James Poniewozik, "Why Reality TV Is Good for Us," *TIME*, February 12, 2003. www.time.com/time/magazine/article/0,9171,421047,00.html.

In 2000, CBS premiered *Survivor* and *Big Brother*, and in 2001, it began airing *The Amazing Race*. *Survivor*, which premiered its 37th season in 2018, features a group of strangers placed in the wilderness, divided into "tribes," and tasked with providing food, water, and shelter for themselves. They also compete in challenges to earn rewards or to gain immunity from being voted off the show by their fellow contestants. The ultimate winner of the show—the last survivor standing—receives a prize of $1 million. *Big Brother*, which premiered its 20th season in 2018, is similar in structure to *The Real World* in that it places a group of strangers together in a house and monitors them constantly with cameras. However, on *Big Brother*, the Houseguests, as they are called, are completely isolated from the outside world and interact only with each another for the three months filming lasts. Each week, votes from the other Houseguests are counted to evict one person from the house, and the contestant who remains at the end wins $500,000. On *The Amazing Race*, teams of two compete in a race around the world, performing various challenges and tasks—everything from skydiving to beard styling—along the way, trying to finish ahead of the other teams. Each episode makes up one leg of the race. Typically, the last team to finish a leg is sent home, and the winning team takes home $1 million. The show finished its 30th season in 2018.

Survivor was so popular after it premiered that it became part of the national consciousness. Even people who did not watch the show could recognize its distinctive logo (shown here).

After the premieres of these three series, reality programming blossomed. *Trading Spaces*, a show in which neighbors swap homes and are given money to remake one room, hit the air in 2000. It originally ran through 2008 and then was revived 10 years later. This influential show was the first major hit in the home makeover subgenre. *The Bachelor*, which features an attractive single man attempting to choose a wife from among a pool of female contestants, appeared in 2002, and its gender-flipped spinoff, *The Bachelorette*, premiered in 2003. Celebrity-based shows took off that same year with the premiere of *The Osbournes*, which followed the family of heavy metal musician Ozzy Osbourne. This show became immensely popular, especially with people who remembered Ozzy from the height of his musical career as the front man of Black Sabbath. Much of what people found appealing about the show was how it imitated a traditional family sitcom in such a funny way. Although in some respects the Osbournes were a typical family, in many ways, they were not. The show was often played for laughs, but it did document some serious events in the lives of the Osbournes, such as Ozzy's wife Sharon's battle with cancer.

American Idol also debuted in 2002, leading a wave of competition shows that included *America's Next Top Model* (2003), *The Apprentice* (2004), *Dancing with the Stars* (2005), and *So You Think You Can Dance* (2005).

Reality TV in Europe

Reality programming is certainly not limited to the United States. In fact, like many scripted American programs based on European shows—including *The Office* and *House of Cards*—many of the best-known American reality shows are versions of programs that began in foreign countries, especially European ones. For example, *Expedition Robinson* debuted in Sweden in 1997 and originally ran until 2005. It was revived from 2009 to 2012, then again for one season in 2015, and was picked up yet again in 2018. This show provided the model for *Survivor*. *Big Brother* actually originated in the Netherlands in 1999. *The Voice* is an adaptation of *The Voice of Holland*. *Dancing with the Stars* is based on the British program *Strictly Come Dancing*. Britain's *Pop Idol*, which first aired in 2001, gave birth to *American Idol*, as well as similar versions in numerous other countries. Indeed, Britain is responsible for a large number of reality television exports; in 2011, 43 percent of global entertainment formats came from that country. Later, however, according to the *Economist*, the British public began to turn away from the typical reality shows that placed cast members in fake environments, instead showing more interest in programs that were less artificial. Two examples are *24 Hours in A&E*, a documentary-style show about events that take place at British hospitals, and *One Born Every Minute*, which focuses on couples who are dealing with childbirth. "Soft-scripted" shows, or programs that mix real behavior with some scripted moments, have also begun to gain popularity. Two such programs are *Made in Chelsea*, which focuses on the young social elite of London's Chelsea district, and *The Only Way Is Essex*, which follows a group of party promoters, models, and club managers in wealthy Essex County outside London. Despite these new interests, however, many of the most-watched reality shows in the United Kingdom (UK) are still titles that are familiar to Americans, such as *The Voice UK* and *Britain's Got Talent*.

Most European countries have their own versions of the most well-known reality shows, such as *Survivor*, *Big Brother*, *MasterChef*, and *American Idol*. However, there are programs that are unique to each country as well. France, for example, has *Rendez-vous en terre inconnue* (*See You in a Strange Land*), in which a group of participants is taken to a secret location and given two weeks to adapt to the native lifestyle. From 2010 to 2012, Germany had *Daniela Katzenberger—Natürlich blond* (*Naturally Blond*), which featured Daniela Katzenberger, a singer and model. Katzenberger's on-camera personality, which has been labeled as "ditzy," has led some to call her the "German Paris Hilton." Australia, which has a culture similar to Europe's due to centuries of colonization, also has its own versions of many popular European and American reality shows.

Asian Reality Programming

Reality programming is readily available in Europe, and it is also very popular in Asian countries. South Korea has produced a fair amount of reality shows, such as *Infinite Challenge*, where contestants competed in weekly challenges that were silly or impossible to achieve. *Running Man* is another popular Korean show that involves contestants traveling all over the world to complete challenges, and *Real Man* follows celebrities who are sent to complete their mandatory Korean military service. Many Koreans, like many Americans, are obsessed with the lives of celebrities, so most of their reality shows revolve around celebrities and how they live their lives in various situations. For instance, a show called *I Live Alone* shows how celebrities live in their homes when they are alone. This is meant to show Koreans how relatable and down-to-earth these celebrities are.

China has its own versions of most of these shows, and Koreans have accused China of plagiarism because they have simply copied the format and title of the shows without actually buying the rights to them. One original Chinese reality show, which has been on the air since 1997, is called *Happy Camp*. It is a variety show that features singers, actors, sports stars, and other celebrities, all participating in activities such as games, interviews, and performances. It is one of the most popular shows on Chinese television.

As for reality television in other Asian countries, Japan is well-known for its wacky game shows, some of which have been adapted for other countries. It also features shows such as Fuji TV's *Ainori Love Wagon*, in which single people travel around the world in a pink bus and try to make romantic connections with each other while learning about other countries.

Shown here is the cast of Korea's Infinite Challenge.
This popular show ran from 2005 to 2018.

Indonesia has also produced many reality programs, although that number has begun to decrease in recent years. Popular shows in that country include *Jika Aku Menjadi* (*If I Were*), which sends wealthy citizens to aid poor Indonesians in rural areas, and *Minta Tolong* (*Ask for Help*), a hidden-camera show similar to the American show *What Would You Do?*, in which people are secretly filmed encountering a controversial scene, such as a mugging setup.

Reality Shows in Arab Countries

Some people are surprised to learn that reality TV even exists in historically conservative Arab countries governed by strict customs about what is appropriate and what is not. Most of these programs seek to appeal to the younger members of the population, who are not afraid to push limits and embrace more progressive values. As Joe Kalil, a communications professor in Qatar, explained, "The shows are trying to say to this young and vibrant group who wants to learn, wants to be entertained: 'This is you. This is your culture. These are your values and your decisions. Make them count.'"9

One of the most popular reality shows in Arab countries is *Star Academy Arab World*, a version of a program that originally aired in Europe. The show, which debuted in 2003, is similar to *American Idol* but has more of a focus on the participants' personal lives and relationships with one another. Contestants are selected from a variety of Arab countries to live together in a penthouse from which footage is continuously aired on a satellite channel and perform weekly for viewer votes. Talent is not limited to singing; some contestants dance or act. Other programs have included a home-makeover show called *Labor and Materials*, in which houses destroyed during the war in Iraq were rebuilt, and even an Arab version of *The Bachelor* and *The Bachelorette* called *ala al-Hawa Sawa*, which roughly translates to *On Air Together*. This show, which aired in 2004, was the first original reality show in the Arab world. It featured "eight women [living] together in a *Big Brother*-style luxury apartment with suitors [potential husbands] able to view the girls 24 hours a day. They were allowed to contact the women before a possible meeting in the flat [apartment] to propose marriage."[10] The show ended in controversy when one of the two remaining women changed her mind about getting married and locked herself in a room right before the finale.

Reality television is a worldwide phenomenon. Many countries have created different versions centered on the same topic with culturally specific twists. Singing competitions are especially popular around the world.

Reality TV in Other Countries

Some reality programs in Africa have also created controversy over what is seen as inappropriate behavior in African cultures. The main complaints have focused on *Big Brother Africa*, which has been accused of presenting immoral behavior to Africa's youth. Unlike most other versions of *Big Brother*, where all the contestants come from one country, *Big Brother Africa* takes at least one contestant from 17 different African countries to live together in the isolated house. African countries offer fewer reality shows than many of their counterparts on other continents, and most of them, such as *Big Brother Africa*, are versions of European shows, including *Survivor: Africa* and several versions of *Idol*. Some original programs exist, however, such as *Ready for*

Marriage Extraordinary, in which former sex workers attempt to find husbands.

Some Central and South American countries feature original programs as well. For example, Mexico has *Iniciativa México* (*Initiative Mexico*), a program that focuses on improving the welfare of the population. On the show, activists compete for $2.5 million to pay for programs they believe will aid the country's poor. Chile created a show called *Mundos Opuestos* (*Opposite Worlds*), which was marketed as a competition between a group living in a split house: one half was futuristic, while the other half simulated life in the past. The groups competed against each other in challenges, and each week, the winners got to choose which side of the house they would live in. In 2012, Brazil debuted the controversial *Mulheres Ricas* (*Rich Women*), which focused on the lives of five of the country's female millionaires. The show created instant debate because the country is one of the most economically unequal societies in the world, and it was canceled in 2013.

Reality television is everywhere in the 21st century. Producers are drawn to reality TV for a variety of reasons. First and foremost, people watch it. There will always be a market for normal people in extraordinary situations. Second, it is much cheaper to produce reality shows than scripted ones, and the production time needed is much shorter. If a show fails, it is cheap and easy to scrap it and make another attempt with another concept. As long as there is a market for it and it remains easy and inexpensive to produce, reality TV will continue to expand.

Why Is Reality Television Popular?

Reality television has been undeniably popular almost since it was first created. While ratings have dropped in recent years, reality shows topped the ratings list of most-watched programs among 18- to 49-year-olds for quite a few years. Although there has been a decrease in viewership, the genre still remains popular. However, along with widespread fascination, there is also widespread contempt for the genre. Many people do not see watching reality TV as a worthwhile way to spend time. These critics tend to view reality shows as lazy and exploitative as well as less thought-provoking or interesting than scripted shows. This has led some people to question who is watching reality programs and what, if any, traits they have in common. Research into this area has shown that reality shows draw viewers from all major statistical groups—age, gender, class, race, and so forth—and studies indicate that people watch reality shows for a variety of reasons.

Relatability

One reason offered for the popularity of reality television is that viewers relate to the contestants because the contestants seem like ordinary people, very much like the viewers themselves. Author Eric Jaffe, commenting on the 51 million viewers who tuned in to the *Survivor* finale in 2000, said, "By watching in such high numbers, viewers told network executives to dump their high-priced writers and lovely actors in favor of identifiable people in familiar conflicts. All we really wanted to see was the same thing we saw in the mirror every morning—ourselves. Only different."[11]

People might also enjoy imagining themselves in the place of the cast members on reality shows. A study published in the *Journal of Consumer Research* in 2005 found that viewers often like to imagine what they would do if placed in the same situation or faced with the same problem as a participant in a reality program they watched. This process of social comparison with the reality participant helps viewers define their own values and beliefs.

Although it is a common claim that people watch reality television because the new American Dream is to become famous even without having any noticeable skill or talent, many scholars disagree. Psychology professor Bryant Paul, for example, believes that the fact that the participants on many reality shows are so ordinary lessens the need for viewers themselves to become famous. According to Paul, "The fact that these [reality show participants] were not groomed for celebrity in the traditional sense, that friends of friends invariably went to camp with someone on one of the shows, is the great draw. The closer someone is to you, the easier it is to empathize … and really good empathy equals really good television."[12]

Seeing Celebrities as Ordinary People

If it is true that people are drawn to reality shows because the participants are not celebrities, what is the explanation for the mass appeal of reality programs that star established celebrities? Shows such as *Very Cavallari*, *Ashlee+Evan*, and *Total Bellas* have drawn viewers curious to peek into the lives of the rich and famous. People are interested in watching celebrities living their day-to-day lives. They draw comfort from the fact that celebrities face many of the same problems ordinary people do, from fights with their friends to challenges in raising kids. Watching celebrities perform everyday tasks helps the average person relate to them and helps viewers feel better about their own lives by letting them know that they are not so far removed from the stars they idolize.

Many of the celebrities who appear on reality shows are lower-tier entertainers that the media invests less time and interest in, which appears to be the way viewers prefer it. This may be

Ashlee+Evan follows Ashlee Simpson and Evan Ross as they live their lives and make music together. Both also have famous musical relatives: Jessica Simpson and Diana Ross.

because major stars are simply seen as too "different" for the average viewer to identify with at all. Many star participants were well-known at some point in the past, but then faded from public view until they popped up unexpectedly on a reality show such as *Dancing with the Stars*.

Another reason why celebrity reality shows draw viewers is because celebrities in general provide a shared cultural experience among members of a population. For example, two people who do not have much in common might be able to bond over their shared love of a particular actor or singer. As Christopher E. Bell pointed out in his book *American Idolatry*, shared cultural references are becoming harder to come by as the number of entertainment options people have increases, making it more difficult for people to bond over one particular book, film, or television show. As Bell put it, "Celebrities provide cultural touchstones at the same time they serve as cultural totems [representations] for how (and how not) to behave."[13]

One shared cultural experience that results in the popularity of a reality show is nostalgia, or longing for a happy past. Producers take advantage of the willingness of viewers to tune in to a show to find out the latest about someone who may have been well-known and well-liked in the past. For example, some viewers were eager to see Ralph Macchio, the star of classic movies such as 1984's *The Karate Kid*, when he competed on *Dancing with the Stars* in 2011. Casting Macchio—who had largely disappeared from the public eye by that time—on the reality program was a calculated move to play on the nostalgia of people who had enjoyed his performances in those 1980s films and were curious about what he was up to in 2011. In general, this show often recruits formerly well-known actors, athletes, singers, and other personalities to pair with ballroom dancing pros and compete against each other, which draws viewers who are eager to see what a particular celebrity looks like or has been up to since dropping out of the spotlight. In recent years, the popularity of this and several other similar shows has resulted in their ability to draw a higher level of celebrity talent than in their early seasons.

SENDING THE WRONG MESSAGE

"Reality television plays to people's worst instincts and depends on people behaving badly, manipulating others, lying and violence."

—Matt Philbin, managing editor of the Media Research Center's Culture and Media Institute

Quoted in Hollie McKay, "Reality Shows Aimed at Young Viewers Airing More Violent Scenes," Fox News, October 11, 2010. www.foxnews.com/entertainment/2010/10/11/reality-shows-battery-domestic-violence-jersey-shore-teen-mom.

Modern-Day Talent Shows

Another reason people watch talent competitions such as *Dancing with the Stars* is more straightforward: They are sometimes rewarded with outstanding performances. For every terrible audition the viewer is forced to endure on *American Idol*, there is someone such as Adam Lambert earning a standing ovation from notoriously cranky judge Simon Cowell for his performance of "Mad World." These are the moments that people talk about the next day at work or school, and viewers are excited to be part of the discussion. This program has produced internationally known superstars as well, such as Kelly Clarkson, the big-voiced winner of the show's first season, and

Carrie Underwood, the country singer who won the fourth season. Even many people who do not come in first, such as Lambert, have found a certain amount of fame if they perform well enough. He joined legendary band Queen in 2011, and although fans say no one will ever replace Queen's original front man Freddie Mercury—who died in 1991 and is the subject of the 2018 movie *Bohemian Rhapsody*—Lambert has been well received as Mercury's stand-in. *The Voice* eliminates the bad auditions altogether, showcasing only those with real talent. *So You Think You Can Dance* also produces moments of brilliance, and its routines are often nominated for Emmys in the category of Best Choreography.

American Idol *launched the careers of many winning and runner-up performers, including Adam Lambert (left).*

In addition to enjoying the performances, viewers also know that with many reality shows, they can directly affect the lives of the participants with their votes. This allows viewers to feel involved in the program and provides a sense of power. Communications professor S. Shyam Sundar, speaking during *American Idol*'s reign at the top of the ratings chart, explained that "the experience feels less like simply watching television and more like being part of a shared national project."[14] Rather than simply watching singers, the viewers become active

The Importance of Planning

It might seem contradictory to think of planning an unscripted show, but if the production team of a reality show is unprepared for all possibilities, things can go disastrously wrong. In some cases, a lack of planning can affect a show's ratings. For example, in 2016, a show called *Eden* aired in Britain. It followed a group of people who lived in the wilderness for a year, but the producers considered it to be an experiment, and, as an article in the *New Yorker* put it, the show seemed "as if it wasn't sure if it was a documentary or something more performative."[1] *Eden* lost viewers almost immediately, and although many of the participants stayed at the campsite for the full year, the show went off the air after only four episodes.

In other circumstances, a lack of planning can affect the participants' health and safety. For instance, an American version of the Chilean show *Opposite Worlds* aired on Syfy in 2014. In a 2018 review of the show, YouTuber Jenny Nicholson explained several problems caused by the producers' failure to account for unexpected events. One of these was the weather. The show was filmed in January near New Orleans, Louisiana; the weather was expected to be warm, but that winter was unusually cold, so the contestants in the "past" half of the house had trouble staying warm and healthy. Another issue was that some of the challenges the players competed in were very dangerous. In the first challenge, players battled with cattle prods on top of a tall platform. Nicholson described how the lack of planning endangered the competitors, with disastrous results for one named Charles: "They have safety cushions, but they're narrow, and they're placed in such a way that they assume that you're gonna just go to the edge and then gently fall straight down. Charles was pushed, so he falls 10 feet onto the ground below and completely misses the safety cushion. He horrifyingly shatters his leg … and has to get taken away by an ambulance."[2] Other competitors got hurt on the show as well. In contrast, shows such as *Survivor* test their challenges repeatedly to make them as safe as possible. While there is always the potential for things to go unexpectedly wrong, the rehearsals of the challenges help reduce this possibility.

1. Sam Knight, "Reality TV's Wildest Disaster," *New Yorker*, September 4, 2017. www.newyorker.com/magazine/2017/09/04/reality-tvs-wildest-disaster.

2. Jenny Nicholson, "The Worst Reality Show of All Time," YouTube video, 25:42, February 6, 2018. www.youtube.com/watch?v=JKFgn6tNU6w.

participants who can help change the lives of those they consider to be worthy.

The Entertainment of Humiliation

Of course, not all performances on these shows are worthy of praise, which is just fine with some viewers. Many people watch out of a sense of pleasure at the misfortune of others, which can perhaps be best simplified as "better them than me." Some people tune in specifically to laugh at bad auditions and failed attempts. They get a sense of personal satisfaction from thinking, "I would never humiliate myself in front of millions of people the way that person is doing."

This attitude highlights another reason why some people watch reality programming of all types—to make fun of the people on the shows and feel superior to them. Many people enjoy sitting in the comfort of their own home and mocking contestants who make mistakes. These viewers tend to feel that in a similar situation, they would make different choices or perform better.

According to clinical psychologist Geoffrey White, viewers enjoy identifying with a cast member who is humiliating another and knowing at the same time that they are not actually responsible for the suffering that results. However, in this day and age, the average viewer is sometimes able to have personal communication, of a sort, with someone on a television show, thanks to social media and the internet. Most reality show participants have Twitter and Instagram accounts that viewers can follow and post comments to. The increasing connection people can have with their favorite celebrities and reality show contestants has sometimes blurred the lines between good-natured teasing and targeted online harassment.

For most people, though, it appears that this focus on others' suffering is less mean-spirited than it seems at first. White also pointed out that in uncertain times, when the population is feeling uneasy or unsettled, seeing that others are suffering as well might serve as a source of comfort. Indeed, many people claim to watch reality television because it makes them feel better about their own lives by allowing them to think, "I may have problems, but at least I'm not hoarding animals or being humiliated on national television." Reality programs help put things in perspective for these viewers, and while they may laugh about the bad decisions made by reality show participants, viewers might also learn from them—and hope the participants will learn something as well. As *Jersey Shore* fan Sydney Lipez admitted, "I do look for redeeming qualities in these people ... and I root for them. I want to find out that they're not as stupid as I think."[15]

Research has also found that not everyone enjoys seeing others embarrassed on television. In one study of the show *Survivor*, the researcher found that of the study participants, "none found appeal in watching cast members being ... voted off the show. In fact, reactions were exactly the opposite, as voiced by this group member: 'Some of the times that seem to trouble me the most is when someone's being humiliated. I don't really like that.'"[16]

Shown here is Nicole "Snooki" Polizzi from Jersey Shore. *Some viewers enjoy watching her and other reality stars in embarrassing situations.*

Media Studies

One of the first important academic studies to focus on reasons why people watch reality television was conducted by communications professor Robin Nabi and her colleagues in 2003. In the study, the researchers investigated whether there was truth to the theory that people watched reality programs to satisfy voyeuristic tendencies. Voyeurism, in this case, was mainly defined as getting an unhealthy level of personal pleasure from peeking into the lives of other people.

The study was conducted on 252 residents of Tucson, Arizona, who appeared for jury duty. The participants completed a survey that measured their personality traits, their overall television viewing patterns, their exposure to several reality television programs, and their thoughts on one particular reality program of which they were either a regular or casual viewer. The top three reasons regular viewers of reality programming gave for watching were that they found the programs entertaining, found the programs suspenseful, and enjoyed the unscripted nature of reality shows. Casual viewers—those who only tuned in to a reality program once in a while—reported that they liked to watch out of a sense of curiosity and for entertainment. A sense of voyeurism, although present to some degree in most viewers, was not found to be the main reason people watched reality programs. Rather than wanting to peek inside people's personal lives out of nosiness, viewers were more interested in feeling connected to others and gaining personal insight about the human condition.

DISLIKED, YET POPULAR

"Keeping Up With the Kardashians ... and the *Real Housewives* franchise ... are ... among the least-liked shows—and also among the highest-rated series on their respective networks, E! and Bravo."

–Rick Porter, writer for *Hollywood Reporter*, reporting on the results of a 2018 *Hollywood Reporter*/Morning Consult poll

Rick Porter, "Most Americans Think There's Too Much Reality TV—but They're Still Watching," *Hollywood Reporter*, November 27, 2018. www.hollywoodreporter.com/live-feed/americans-think-reality-tv-but-theyre-still-watching-1164205.

A second study by Nabi, along with Carmen Stitt, Jeff Halford, and Keli Finnerty, was published in *Media Psychology* in 2006. Nabi and her colleagues built upon their past research as well as studies done by other researchers. They examined whether the motivations for watching reality programs differed from those for watching fictional programs and how the enjoyment of viewers of reality television differed according to the type of reality program they watched.

Stereotypes about Reality TV Viewers

A 2018 poll by the *Hollywood Reporter* and Morning Consult revealed that reality TV is the only genre that a majority of the respondents viewed negatively and said there was too much of. Many people who prefer to think of themselves as intelligent and cultured look down on reality TV and those who enjoy it. Some people who consider themselves to have these traits feel embarrassed by the enjoyment they get out such shows and feel a need to explain to themselves and others why they continue to watch. Some viewers consider reality TV to be a guilty pleasure that they are allowed to indulge in as long as they do not do it all the time. Others say they watch it ironically; according to interviews conducted by the website The Conversation, these people "derive great pleasure from making fun of a terrible show … Watching with this perspective allows them to feel superior to the show and its conventional viewers,"[1] or those who actually get invested in the people and scenarios on the shows.

A third reason people gave for excusing their reality TV viewing was that they experienced a "camp sensibility," or "a strange kind of admiration—almost reverence—for really awful cultural products."[2] In contrast to ironic viewers, people with a camp sensibility do not hate the shows for being bad, they love them for it. People who do not think of themselves as more cultured or intelligent than the rest of the population do not tend to feel as much of a need to excuse themselves for liking reality TV. This illustrates that reality shows appeal to a wide variety of people, despite their negative reputation.

1. Charles McCoy and Roscoe Scarborough, "The Guilty Pleasure of Watching Trashy TV," The Conversation, May 20, 2015, theconversation.com/the-guilty-pleasure-of-watching-trashy-tv-40214.
2. McCoy and Scarborough, "The Guilty Pleasure of Watching Trashy TV."

Again, the participants of the study were residents of Tucson, Arizona, who had reported for jury duty. Because of the small, localized sample size, these results may not necessarily be true for a wider population, but since few studies of this kind have been done, the results give a good starting point for understanding people's motivations when watching reality TV. Half of the participants received surveys asking them about fictional programming they watched, and the other half received surveys asking about reality programming. One of the questions on both surveys asked viewers to list the emotions and reactions they tended to experience when watching the programming in question (both fictional and reality).

The study found that people did not watch reality programming to experience pleasure through voyeurism, judge others, or compare themselves to people on the shows (social comparison) any more than they did for fictional programming. For reality programming, experiencing curiosity, happiness, surprise, and relief increased enjoyment of these shows, while experiencing anger lessened it.

The study also indicated that different types of reality programs offered viewers different types of enjoyment. For example, romance-based reality programs such as *The Bachelor*

People are more emotionally invested in the lives of people that they see as "real," or genuine, regardless of how manipulated the circumstances surrounding most reality programs are. One example is Becca Kufrin, whom people invested in on both The Bachelor *and* The Bachelorette. *She is shown here with Garrett Yrigoyen, whom she picked as the winning contestant on* The Bachelorette.

were enhanced by voyeurism, whereas talent-based programs such as *American Idol* rated high in the enjoyment of judging others and of parasocial relationships—those in which only one of the people involved knows a great deal about the other, such as the relationship between a celebrity and a fan. However, the strongest predictor of enjoyment across all the reality show subgroups—except for the romance subgroup—was happiness. Nabi and her colleagues concluded, "It appears that the enjoyment people [get] from watching others, that is, our [natural] curiosity about the human condition in its various forms, is an important component to the appeal and enjoyment of [reality programming] and one that distinguishes reality from fictional programming."[17] In other words, people enjoy watching things that seem real. Seeing real people interact, live, and love one another is more rewarding than seeing actors do the same thing. Viewers feel more connected and invested in the lives of people they see as "real."

It is also important to note that studies have found no relationship between either intelligence level or physical activity and the viewing of reality programs. This finding conflicts with common beliefs that people who watch reality programs are of below-average intelligence and are physically inactive. These are stereotypes with no basis in reality.

Start Getting "Real"

Today, most people are well aware that reality television somewhat stretches the definition of the word "reality." This knowledge, however, does not necessarily prevent someone from enjoying a show. In fact, while watching a show, it is sometimes difficult for people to keep in mind that what happened behind the scenes is not necessarily what they are seeing in front of them. While most reality programs do not have a script for people to memorize, it is certainly not as simple as gathering people together and pointing a camera at them. People may be surprised to learn exactly how much manipulation goes on behind the scenes to create a watchable show.

Casting

The manipulation of a reality show begins early, in the casting stage. Applicants for many reality programs must go through an exhaustive process that may involve making videotapes of themselves, numerous interviews, background checks, psychological testing, and even physical examinations. In most situations, casting directors work to fill certain "roles" and to find a particular mix of personalities—and they frequently look for people whose personalities they know will clash. Shows commonly seek out cast members that fit certain stereotypes or categories, such as the "bad boy" or the "party girl." The ethnicity, race, gender, and sexual orientation of possible participants are taken into consideration for shows that want to have diverse cast members.

Casting directors are not alone, however, in the effort to fill roles with interesting characters. Hopeful contestants have been able to figure out, in general, what producers are looking for and adjust their personalities accordingly for auditions. Numerous resources exist that reality show hopefuls can consult for auditioning tips, including websites, books, and even classes and workshops. With this in mind, the notion that cast members are "real" people just looking to be themselves is sometimes hard to believe.

Psychological testing can help the producers make sure they can provide a balanced and interesting show. An interview with Richard Levak, a psychologist who has worked on programs such as *Survivor* and *The Apprentice*, revealed,

> *If you put 16 conflict-avoiders together on an island … you won't end up with very interesting TV. On the other hand, if you compose a group entirely with aggressive, [outgoing], Type A personalities, you may produce some fireworks, but it's unlikely you'll [keep] an audience's attention over weeks. Instead, the most compelling viewing comes when people with different yet recognizable personalities evolve over time in relation to those around them while dealing with competition and [difficult] circumstances.*[18]

LETTING A REALITY SHOW MAKE THE CHOICE

"The idea of turning the decision like that over to experts seemed to make a lot of sense … It feels like a dream come true for people to say, *Wow, I get to take all the stress out of it and I just give it all over to someone else.*"

–Chris Coelen, CEO of Kinetic Content, on why people sign up for shows that make major life decisions for them

Quoted in Andy Dehnart, "Would You Let a Reality Show Pick Your Home? Or Your Spouse?," Vulture, November 9, 2018. www.vulture.com/2018/11/buying-it-blind-married-at-first-sight-reality-tv.html

Psychological exams can also give producers a clue about how a show's participants will react to a situation or challenge. This gives producers a chance to plan out the show for maximum drama and to avoid surprises once filming begins. After the casting is complete, participants are required to sign very long contracts, some of which give reality show producers the right to make up anything they like about the cast member as long as they think it will make for good TV. Megan Parris, a contestant on season 13 of *The Bachelor*, explained, "You'll hear someone make one comment and then they'll show a clip of somebody's face to make it look like that is their facial reaction to that statement, but really, somebody made that face the day before to something else … It's just piecing things together to make a story."[19]

What Is Being "Real"?

Once the cast of a reality program has been set and filming begins, the participants may or may not be showing their real personalities in front of the cameras. Several memorable reality show participants, such as Richard Hatch—the first winner of *Survivor*—and *The Apprentice*'s Omarosa Manigault Newman, said after their seasons were over that they were very aware of the cameras and were playing to them. Manigault Newman, who is one of reality television's best-known "villains," told one reporter that she had followed the advice of a friend who said, "The fabric of reality TV is conflict, so make sure that you're either in the fight, breaking the fight up, or starting the fight."[20] Likewise, Hatch claimed that viewers saw his "game face" and not his real personality during *Survivor*.

Other reality show cast members have made similar claims. Screenwriter Anna Klassen wrote an article for *Bustle* about a reality show pilot she had filmed, explaining that she knew she was being asked to play a character: "It was clear what character the producers wanted me to play. They were casting the stereotypical L.A. girl: Long blonde hair, thin, perhaps a bit shallow, and with a small, fluffy dog to boot."[21]

It is possible that some of these claims are a form of damage control once the show is over; after all, nobody wants to come across as stupid or cruel. However, in some cases, participants on a program have agreed that their fellow cast members acted differently on camera. According to Derek Woodruff, a contestant on a florists' competition called *The Arrangement*, "Personally, I know that I was true to myself on and off camera, but I know for a fact that some of the other contestants put on their stage face for the camera, because in person, they were not like that at all."[22]

For some people, the knowledge that they are being filmed for TV changes their personality to a certain degree.

Despite all this, show producers claim that what the viewer sees is ultimately the real thing, especially in the case of shows such as *Big Brother* or *The Real World*, which feature constant monitoring of the cast members. Mary-Ellis Bunim, co-creator of *The Real World* and *Road Rules*, once insisted, "You can't sustain a character that isn't true to yourself day and night, for thirteen weeks. It's just not possible. It would drive you mad."[23] Producers have an incentive, of course, to promote the reality of the product they are putting out. However, some cast members agree that personality can only be faked to a certain degree. Burton Roberts, who appeared on the third season of *Survivor*, was a former Eagle Scout who had already participated in other outdoor challenges—a perfect fit for the show. According to Roberts, "My strategy in the first week was to lay low, to not stand out, and to try not to be a leader under any circumstances.

That lasted a whole six hours … At the end of the day, you're pretty much who you are, and that will come out."[24] Former *Apprentice* contestant Sam Solovey had a slightly different perspective: "People accused me of playing to the cameras, but I don't think I did. I think the cameras draw the extremes of your personality out. If you're shy, the cameras make you more shy. If you're someone who loves an audience, they push you in that direction."[25]

However, some producers, including Bunim's former creative partner Jonathan Murray, have admitted that their shows have become harder to cast, partly because young people raised on reality television now come in knowing which "character" they want to play on the show. It became a loop: People who grew up watching reality TV auditioned to be on reality programs and behaved the way they saw people on reality shows behaving. Murray stressed that what producers really want are honest, complex personalities who have not figured out their lives yet, not those who seek to be on a reality show to become famous or start acting careers. As a result, some producers, such as Thom Beers of *Deadliest Catch* and *Storage Wars*, search for cast members in ways other than casting calls or audition tapes. Beers claimed he liked to find people through friends of friends or from messages he saw on Facebook or Craigslist, because, as he put it, "Normal people aren't necessarily there looking for fame but more likely looking for a slightly used mattress."[26]

Make It Happen

Cast members looking for fame and attention—either positive or negative—are not the only issues that affect the filming of a reality show. There are many ways that producers might manipulate a show. Producers control everything from the environment in which the contestants are placed to the final cut of what eventually ends up being shown on the air.

Once filming has ended and the show has aired, reality show participants are generally free to discuss the circumstances of the show, and often, what they say proves to be rather illuminating. Some have claimed that producers used various methods to influence their behavior on camera. As most reality cast members are not represented by a labor union, they do not have the same protections and rights given to actors on scripted shows. This means producers can legally treat them in ways that might endanger their physical and mental health. Participants on *Project Runway* and *Hell's Kitchen* have said they were almost completely shut off from the outside world and only allowed a few hours of sleep every night. This left them stressed and too tired to function well, which of course led to temper flare-ups and people exhibiting volatile behavior that they might not have normally.

Reality show contestants often do not know each other prior to filming, which can lead to awkward exchanges. Nobody wants to watch strangers making small talk, which is why producers often give contestants a lot of alcohol. In some cases, alcohol has also been provided to fire up the behavior of cast members. One *New York Times* article reported that "during the 2006 season of the popular ABC dating show *The Bachelor*, the contestants waited in vans for several hours while the crew set up for a 12-hour 'arrival' party where, two contestants said, there was little food but bottomless glasses of wine. When producers judged the [action] too boring, they sent out a production assistant with a tray of shots."[27]

CREATING DRAMA

"The producers have a big role in what's happening on the show. They create a lot of drama and they start a lot of the fights ... they will say so and so said this about you behind your back, and she said she slept with your boyfriend. It's like high school."

—Jayde Nicole, former cast member on
The Hills and *Holly's World*

Quoted in Andrea Canning and Elizabeth Stuart, "Reality Show Violence Getting Too Real?," ABC News, March 30, 2011. abcnews.go.com/Entertainment/reality-tv-show-violence-real-life-consequences-teen/story?id=13256971

If producers cannot spark the drama they want by keeping cast members tired and giving them alcohol, they might become even more directly involved. In a 2008 interview, one *Bachelor* producer revealed,

> *Well, in the private one-on-one interviews with a producer (like me) it is [my] job to get the [trash talk] started, like "tell me honestly what you think of Sally"—if the interviewee does not want to respond in a catty way then the producer will usually go to the next level, like "well I personally think she is a self absorbed, attention starved skank," and then see if the person will take the bait. Once you start learning who in the house is not well liked it is easy to start seeding conversations and gossip.*[28]

The producer also admitted that food or rewards were sometimes withheld from contestants unless the contestants gave them the type of comments they wanted. Although people are aware that this kind of thing happens, it is sometimes hard for viewers to remember when they do not see it happen. This often leads people to make assumptions about the cast that might not be true. As journalist Dustin Grinnell noted, "if someone stocked your cabinets with booze and shacked you up in a spiffy mansion without televisions and phones while you were jobless, isolated from the world and [competing] for one man or woman's heart, you might start trouble, too. You might gossip,

Producers frequently go to great lengths to stir up drama among reality show casts such as the women of the various Real Housewives *shows (shown here).*

overreact, pick a fight … as the man who gives you butterflies kisses your new best friend."[29]

Creative Editing

If the producers still do not get the results they hope for, they can simply edit footage of the cast members to have it say or show whatever they like. They are allowed to do this because the participants sign over the right for producers to do whatever they want with their image and the footage they record. One editing method is known as "frankenbiting." In this process, bits and pieces of audio commentary by a cast member are spliced, or joined, together to create a new sentence that may be completely contrary to what the person originally said. *TIME* magazine gave an example of this that occurred on ABC's *The Dating Game*. According to the article, one of the female cast members did not like the male cast member the producers wanted her to like. When the crew was taping an interview with the woman, they asked who her favorite celebrity was. She responded that she really loved Adam Sandler. Later, the editor spliced out Sandler's name and replaced it with audio of the woman saying the male cast member's name.

Editing tricks can be visual as well. In the same *TIME* article, Jeff Bartsch, a freelance reality show editor, said that scenes are sometimes shown out of order or context (the set of details or facts that surround a particular event) to add more drama. He mentioned the show *Blind Date* and explained how the editing in one episode made it appear that a male participant was having a bad time on his date by showing scenes of him looking bored and unfocused while the woman was talking. In reality, those shots of him had been filmed while his date was in the restroom. Many reality show cast members throughout the years have complained about such editing, saying that the producers spliced footage in ways that made them look like villains. Although it is difficult to argue with this when it comes to examples such as the one on *Blind Date*, other times, the producers insist they are simply working with what they are given by the cast members. In the words of one producer, "If you did it and it got caught on film, it doesn't matter how much other delightful stuff you did—you can't blame the editors for using the good stuff, and you can't claim they [made it up]."[30] Another producer, Mark Cronin, explained that it is very hard to tell a story that did not happen. This is a scenario with a lot of opportunity for continuity error because once a producer starts changing the basic truth—for example, creating a relationship between two people—the producer then has to be aware of *all* the interactions between those two people for the rest of the show. They will have to continue to edit these interactions so they continue to support the fake story the producer has created. Cronin said that all this trouble is generally not worth the effort to producers, so they are unlikely to make major changes to a storyline.

WHY DO REALITY SHOWS NEED EDITORS?

"Who wants to watch people text or browse Facebook? Not entertaining. Editors exist because we need curators. Selectors. We need professionals to ... give us the 'good stuff,' that 1% that dazzles us, holds our eyeballs ... The selectors juxtapose a contestant's remarks with contradictory actions, creating a rich subtext. She said she hates her, but now she's acting pleasant. He said he has a girlfriend, but now he's playing single."

—Dustin Grinnell, journalist

Dustin Grinnell, "We Know Reality TV Is Fake. So Why Do We Treat It Like It's Real?" Thought Catalog, November 2, 2017, thoughtcatalog.com/dustin-grinnell/2017/11/we-know-reality-tv-is-fake-so-why-do-we-treat-it-like-its-real/

Not all reality shows need to be manipulated and edited in order to tell a cohesive, interesting story. Partially, this depends on what the producers want the show to achieve. For example, an anonymous reality TV editor explained to BuzzFeed that the show *Intervention*, in which people were confronted by their loved ones about their substance abuse, was not heavily manipulated because it focused on one dramatic moment in a person's life. In contrast, a show that follows people for long periods of time may have to edit more to get interesting footage.

The Hills: A Surprising Series Finale

The reality show *The Hills* ran for a total of six seasons, from 2006 to 2010. It focused, as *Entertainment Weekly* jokingly wrote, on "two blond girls who live in a nice apartment complex in West Hollywood and pretend to go to work sometimes."[1] Following their jobs, relationships, and other aspects of their lives, it seemed like a typical reality show: Some people loved it, others hated it, and many regarded it as a guilty pleasure. However, it received much criticism during its run for appearing too scripted, even though the producers insisted that everything was real.

This insistence was what made the series finale surprising to many fans. As Kristin, one of the stars of the show, said goodbye to her on-again-off-again boyfriend Brody and rode away in a chauffeured car, the scene suddenly changed. The camera pulled back to reveal that the whole thing was a stage set. Kristin got out of the car and the crew came out from behind the scenes. Brody later explained, "Well that's one of the questions that was always asked in the show, 'Is it real or is it fake?' And we kinda left everybody with 'Well you'll never know what's real and what's fake.'"[2] Although many viewers had suspected *The Hills* was at least partially scripted, they were still surprised to see the show admit it.

1. Emily Exton, "The Hills' Series Finale: The Joke's on Us, Apparently," *Entertainment Weekly*, July 14, 2010. ew.com/article/2010/07/14/the-hills-series-finale-the-jokes-on-us-apparently/
2. Quoted in Exton, "The Hills' Series Finale."

Occasionally, producers will tell cast members what to say and how to act. For example, when *Jersey Shore* was filming in Italy in 2011, several locals and extras reported seeing rehearsals of scenes as well as reshoots from different camera angles, with the cast members repeating the same dialogue over and over. Producers can even manipulate the outcome of competition shows—or at least they can try. The anonymous editor who spoke to BuzzFeed described a design competition show he declined to name:

[A]s the show went on, the network became aware of what characters viewers were responding to, and the actual competition got lost and it was just like, "who do we want to kick off this week? How can we manipulate things so one person leaves or one person stays?" One season the winner was supposed to win their own show, and the network continuously kept this cast member who was far less qualified and far less intelligent than the others but who was cute and bubbly and filled a demographic niche they were looking to fill for a host on their network. By the end the network got their way, and she won. But it turned out she had just gotten pregnant, but they were like, "oh, we don't want a pregnant lady." They worked it out somehow with her—she never got a show.[31]

Who Really Chooses the Winner?

It is a common theory among fans of reality competition programs that the producers have favorites—contestants that they want to continue on the show because their personalities are interesting or controversial. Such claims are hardly new to reality television. In the 1950s, the industry was rocked by quiz show scandals that involved several programs. Those scandals resulted in amendments to the Communications Act of 1934 that made it a crime to rig contests—but only contests of "intellectual knowledge or intellectual skill," such as traditional game shows. Reality show competitions do not appear to be included in the law's scope. Most shows have reserved the right to change the process of crowning a winner at will, based on what will lead to the highest ratings or the most buzz—for example, the website for *So You Think You Can Dance* states, "Voting rules and procedures are subject to change at Producers' sole discretion and without notice."[32]

The producers, however, insist that this is simply a safety measure in case something goes wrong with the call-in voting system. According to producer Nigel Lythgoe, "Whenever you do a contract, you have to anticipate every angle, because you can't tell what's going to happen." He also insisted that rigging a contest would be a foolish move, saying, "The minute you take away somebody the public's voting for, you're [messing] with the program ... There's no logic to [interfering]."[33]

BROADENING HORIZONS

"Reality TV can be educational and realistic. Shows like *The Amazing Race* widen viewers' knowledge about travel and different cultures around the globe, presenting amazing landscapes and history in a fun and addictive way people can learn from."

–Meghan Pilkington, 12th grader from New Zealand

Meghan Pilkington, "A Dose of Reality Can Be Good—in Moderation," *New Zealand Herald,* September 20, 2011. www.nzherald.co.nz/college-herald/news/article.cfm?c_id=1502920&objectid=10753863.

Although producers always dispute the idea that shows are rigged or fixed, accusations continue. After the current wave of reality programming began in the early 2000s, one of the first charges of vote rigging involved *Survivor*. In 2001, a former contestant named Stacey Stillman filed a lawsuit against CBS and the show's producer, Mark Burnett, claiming that Burnett told two other contestants to vote her off the show. Burnett and CBS countersued Stillman for $5 million for harming the show's reputation and breaking her contract. They claimed, in part, that she had broken the 83-page confidentiality agreement she had signed before the show began filming. (Confidentiality agreements, which almost all reality show cast members must sign, say that a cast member cannot reveal certain things about the filming of a show until a set amount of time has passed.) The case was eventually settled out of court.

American Idol has faced similar accusations of rigging nearly every season. One notable example occurred in 2008 when judge Paula Abdul gave her comments on contestant Jason Castro's song before he actually performed it. This led some to suspect that the judges' comments are set before they even see the performances or are fed to them by the show's producers. Abdul denied this, claiming that she had seen Castro perform the song in dress rehearsal and had made notes for the show but accidentally read the wrong notes.

In 2008, Jason Castro (shown here) was involved in accusations that American Idol *was rigged.*

Claims of vote rigging often concern the call-in systems that the programs use to collect viewer votes. If a program is massively popular, call-ins can flood the system and lead to technical issues or busy signals. ABC did admit that its online and telephone voting system was swamped by a record amount of traffic one week during a 2010 season of *Dancing with the Stars*. However, ABC insisted that all three finalists were affected equally and that the problem was quickly corrected. The amount of time allowed for people to cast votes was not extended despite the problem, however, and some people may have run out of time before they were able to place a vote again. Others might simply have given up after their first attempt was unsuccessful. This did not help matters for ABC in a season already full of viewer complaints.

Other claims of call-in system issues affecting competition outcomes have involved *American Idol*. For example, in 2006, some callers dialing in for popular contestant Chris Daughtry were surprised to hear fellow contestant Katharine McPhee's message thanking them for their votes. Daughtry was eliminated the following night, and many of his fans blamed the call-in error.

No voting system is perfect. There will be technical issues as well as people trying to manipulate the system. Producers of reality programs have always been insistent that these kinds of issues have been relatively small in scope and have never affected the eventual outcome of a competition.

CHAPTER 4

Positives and Negatives

Although it is clear that reality shows are not always completely real, fans of other questionably real content, such as professional wrestling and mockumentaries (fictionalized documentaries), can attest to the fact that people can enjoy something even if they know it has been manipulated. A larger problem facing reality TV is that the genre has a terrible reputation. People accuse it of everything from inspiring young people to behave stupidly and cruelly to encouraging teenagers to get pregnant in order to get on television. Parents' organizations often speak out against reality TV and claim it is destroying the morals of today's children and teens.

Others point out that this same behavior can also be found on scripted shows and say it is unfair to place so much of the blame on reality television. In a 2003 article for *TIME*, James Poniewozik explained, "When a reality show [presents] bad behavior, it's immoral … sexist or sick. When *The Sopranos* does the same thing, it's [good] storytelling."[34] So where does the truth lie? Is reality TV harming society?

Aggression and Reality TV

One major criticism aimed at reality TV is that it contains too much violence. In the last decade, many media scholars have noted an increase in incidents of assaults on reality shows. For instance, in a 2010 episode of *Jersey Shore*, Mike "The Situation" Sorrentino slapped fellow cast member Snooki in the face and called it a "love tap." More recently, the 2017 season of *Bachelor in Paradise* had to have production shut down after a concerned producer reported allegations of sexual assault.

More common than physical violence, though, is relational aggression, which includes bullying, excluding people from a certain social group, or manipulating them. Reality TV is known for backstabbing and bullying by people of all genders. It can be seen on competition shows, where people say they came to win the competition rather than to make friends with the rest of the cast, but it can also frequently be seen on shows that follow a cast of housemates. National Public Radio (NPR) used the first episode of *Jersey Shore* as an example: Mere moments after being introduced, "Snooki has already questioned JWoww's sexual morals. Vinny is calling Snooki stupid. The new family is already getting gossipy and aggressive."[35] This kind of disrespect, combined with the large amounts of alcohol reality show casts typically consume, can increase the risk of physical violence.

Some worry that if young people look to reality stars as role models, they might imitate the violence and aggression they see from these stars. When so many people are rewarded for bad behavior with opportunities for fame, it is not difficult to see why this is a concern. According to psychologist Stacey Kaiser, "Things that we used to look away from are things that we watch on television on a daily basis ... It sends a message to viewers that

Many reality shows feature people, such as the cast of Jersey Shore *(shown here), being gossipy and rude to each other. Studies have shown that watching a lot of this type of relational aggression can have a negative influence on viewers.*

it's something that's socially acceptable to our society these days."[36] Several studies have found that watching a lot of aggressive behavior on TV tends to make people more aggressive in real life. Other people disagree that reality shows in particular are the problem, pointing out that scripted shows such as *Riverdale* tend to have a lot of relational aggression as well.

MAKING SHOWS TO MAKE MONEY

"We have no obligation to make history; we have no obligation to make art; we have no obligation to make a statement; to make money is our only objective."

–Michael Eisner, former CEO of Disney/ABC and current owner of media firm The Tornante Company

Quoted in Laurie Ouellette and James Hay, *Better Living Through Reality Television: Television and Post-Welfare Citizenship.* New York, NY: Blackwell, 2008, p. 34.

Body Image and Reality TV

People on reality shows are often obsessed with the way they look, and some shows focus specifically on changing those looks. This has caused some people to become concerned that certain reality programs might make people feel bad about how they look. Judith Orloff, a professor of psychiatry at the University of California, Los Angeles (UCLA), said of shows such as the *Real Housewives* franchise, "These shows can ... be very destructive if younger people watch them. They're getting the message, 'You'll be happy if you ... get a nose job or a face lift.' That's all false."[37]

A study published by Charlotte and Patrick Markey in the academic journal *Body Image* in 2010 found that watching reality television seemed to play a role in convincing young people to get cosmetic surgery. The researchers polled 200 men and women with an average age of 20 about their reactions to shows that focus on body makeovers. The study found that the women were more likely to consider plastic surgery than the men. It also found that those who watched makeover shows were more likely to consider getting plastic surgery than those who watched other shows. According to the American Society of Plastic Surgeons, although adults tend to get plastic surgery to stand out from others, young people tend to want to get rid of certain physical characteristics so they will look more similar to their peers. The article in *Body Image* stated that there is no definite proof that plastic surgery makes people happier. Nevertheless, there are people who have appeared on body-altering shows who say they are glad they did and that their lives have changed for the better. Fashion makeover shows have faced some similar controversy for insulting people's wardrobes and trying to make people fit one particular mold, but overall, they tend to be seen as less objectionable than plastic surgery shows because the changes are not permanent and do not involve risky medical procedures.

PROMOTING OBSESSIVE BEHAVIOR

"The real problem in focusing on our bodies, and on revenge, is that both lend themselves to obsessive behavior ... That might make great television, but is not a viable strategy for coping with loss and rejection. The best medicine for that is time, self-discovery, and understanding our relationship patterns so that we are less likely to repeat them."

–Tabitha Limotte, therapist and eating disorder specialist, in a criticism of *Revenge Body with Khloe Kardashian*

Quoted in Bibi Deitz, "5 Reasons to Boycott Khloe Kardashian's New Show, 'Revenge Body,'" StyleCaster, 2016. stylecaster.com/boycott-khloe-kardashian-revenge-body/.

Weight-loss shows are also generally less controversial than those that focus on cosmetic surgery. The goal of increasing someone's health by reducing obesity is less objectionable to many than changing someone's physical appearance surgically. Obesity is a legitimate health concern, whereas wanting a differently shaped nose typically is not. However, weight-loss shows have faced their share of criticism, mainly because of how they affect the participants. Sometimes people who leave these shows are able to continue living healthy lifestyles and keep the weight off, but overwhelmingly often, since the underlying issues leading to their overeating remain largely unaddressed, they quickly gain the weight back.

A 2016 study from the National Institutes of Health (NIH) followed 14 former contestants of *The Biggest Loser*. Of these 14 participants, the study found that 13 had regained a significant portion of the weight they had lost while on the show—in fact, 4 of those 13 were actually heavier at the time of the study than they had been before they appeared on the show. Experts say that losing weight quickly by making drastic diet and exercise changes did not allow the show's contestants to make permanent healthy changes in their habits, which led most of them to go back to their old habits when the show was over. *The Biggest Loser* and other similar weight-loss competition shows have also been heavily criticized for the strict diet and exercise routines the contestants are put through, which unhealthily

After The Biggest Loser *went off the air, its creator announced a new show called* The Big Fat Truth, *which aims to find out why so many former* Biggest Loser *contestants gained their weight back after the show. This show has received accusations of blaming the former contestants for their choices instead of acknowledging the unhealthy weight-loss methods they went through.*

push them to their physical limits. It was not uncommon for competitors on *The Biggest Loser* to vomit because of how hard they were pushing themselves, which did not set a good example for viewers. Experts say these extreme methods also damaged their metabolism, making it much easier for them to gain weight. Nutritionists have instead pointed to healthier weight-loss shows, such as *Strong* and *I Used to Be Fat*.

Gender Stereotypes on Reality TV

Many reality shows are accused of playing up the worst stereotypes of both men and women. Many critics agree that women are often made to look catty, jealous, desperate, and unintelligent on reality shows—particularly in romantic dating shows such as *The Bachelor*. Women are also sometimes portrayed as less intelligent or capable than men. For example, on *The Real Housewives of Atlanta*, one of the women seemed to be unable to spell the word "cat." Similarly, men on shows such as *Survivor* and *Big Brother* tend to display what experts call "toxic masculinity." They are frequently aggressive, quick to anger, selfish, and cruel. Other men are portrayed as incompetent.

However, supporters point out that some shows do not play into those stereotypes. Strong, capable women can be seen on many reality shows, such as *The Amazing Race* and *Survivor*. *The First 48* often features female homicide detectives who use their intelligence and skills to lead murder investigations. There are also shows—including *Queer Eye* and *Top Chef*—featuring men who are kind, intelligent, patient, and have multifaceted personalities. The way genders are portrayed can play a large role in determining which shows a person chooses to watch.

Race and Sexuality on Reality TV

As in real life, people of color are often treated very badly by reality TV producers and editors. At times, stereotypes of people of color are used to entertain viewers. According to the *Daily*

Beast, "From Oxygen's *Bad Girls* to Bravo's *Real Housewives* franchise, the small screen is awash with black females who roll their eyes, bob their heads, snap their fingers, talk trash, and otherwise reinforce the ugly stereotype of the 'angry black woman.'"[38] Some criticize the way black men are portrayed—as angry, violent, lazy, or unintelligent. Asian and Latinx people are also frequently shown playing up their races' stereotypes. Producers of shows such as *The Real World* and *Big Brother*, however, defend their programs by saying that they address, rather than avoid, racial issues in ways other shows do not and break down barriers by having people of different races living and working closely together. Additionally, some nonwhite cast members have stated that it is unfair to expect them to represent their entire race, saying that viewers should recognize that just because they see one person behaving a certain way, they should not assume all people of that race behave that way.

WHY DO PEOPLE WANT TO BE ON REALITY SHOWS?

"Did I want my husband to see me on television as a kitchen goddess creature brought into existence for a moment? Yes, I did. I wanted to be more special than a person. That impulse alone is both questionable and problematic for a person weighing the odds of a dangerous decision. And I imagine it's a feeling shared by most people wanting to be reality stars."

—Jessie Glenn, former *MasterChef* contestant

Jessie Glenn, "I Am a MasterChef Survivor," *Salon*, February 18, 2018. www.salon.com/2018/02/17/i-am-a-master-chef-survivor/.

Stereotypes are not the only racial issues in reality programming. People of color are often underrepresented on romance reality shows: *The Bachelor* franchise has been on in one version or another since 2002, but the first Bachelor of Latin descent—a man named Juan Pablo Galavis—was not chosen until 2014. Additionally, the contestants are very rarely people of color. Some believe this is because the producers want to avoid tampering with the series' winning formula and fear how people might react to an interracial romance. The creator of these shows, however, claimed this is not true, saying, "We always want to cast for ethnic diversity … It's just that for whatever reason, they don't come forward. I wish they would."[39] In 2012, at least two black men did attend a *Bachelor* casting event; however, those men filed a lawsuit against the show after they were not chosen. Their lawsuit argued that they were never seriously considered for casting due to their race. This lawsuit was ultimately dismissed. Cable shows such as VH1's *Flavor of Love* and *I Love New York* have featured a black main love interest and a greater number of nonwhite contestants, but those shows were also

targeted for supporting racist stereotypes. Former VH1 executive Michael Hirschorn responded to this criticism by pointing out that the shows were more popular with black viewers than white ones.

Other minority groups are also concerned about issues of stereotyping and representation. Shows featuring the LGBT+ community still sometimes have problems to resolve, but they have come a long way since *An American Family*'s Lance Loud received death threats when he became the first openly gay person on television. Early reality shows structured around LGBT+ people were often problematic in terms of the treatment of their participants. For example, in

In 2017, Rachel Lindsay became the first black Bachelorette. The show has been on the air since 2003.

Bravo's 2003 *Boy Meets Boy*, a gay bachelor believed he was looking for a boyfriend from among a group of other gay men but was unaware that half the men were straight and seeking to fool him. Although this show is notable for being one of the first mainstream portrayals of LGBT+ culture, the "twist" reveals how much many producers still had to learn about equal treatment.

THINKING CRITICALLY ABOUT REALITY TV

"I think [reality TV] offers an opportunity for parents and adults working with youth to use these types of programs as a jumping off point to talk about race and racism ... I think ... a dose of reality would help bring these issues to the surface."

–Anastasia Goodstein, senior vice president of digital and social strategy at the Advertising Council

Anastasia Goodstein, "The 'Reality' of Race in America," *Huffington Post,* May 25, 2011.
www.huffingtonpost.com/anastasia-goodstein/the-reality-of-race-in-am_b_37922.html.

Fortunately for the LGBT+ community, *Queer Eye for the Straight Guy* premiered the same year. It became very popular and helped society become more comfortable with seeing openly gay people on television. It originally ran from 2003 to 2006 but was rebooted with a shortened title on Netflix in 2018. Since then, many television shows that focus on the LGBT+ community have hit the airwaves—most notably, *RuPaul's Drag Race*. Additionally, contestants on many reality competition shows, such as *Project Runway* and *The Voice*, are openly gay. *America's Next Top Model* featured a transgender contestant, as did *The Real World: Brooklyn*. In 2018, the Miss Universe pageant featured its first transgender contestant after changing its policy in 2012 to allow transgender women to compete.

Children and Reality TV

While people of color and the LGBT+ community struggle with the ways they are portrayed on reality shows, they are at least all adults who chose to participate in the shows. Different concerns arise when the show centers on children. According to Child AbuseWatch, children on reality shows are considered "participants" rather than "actors," so they are not protected by child labor laws in the same way children who appear in scripted shows are. This means they are not subject to the same restrictions on working hours and general welfare guidelines. Parents are expected to oversee their children's welfare and decide whether or not they should participate. Children—especially younger ones—often have no say in the matter. Many people worry that children might be damaged, either physically or mentally, from participation on a reality show.

Other concerns focus more on the possible effects on a child's mental health and emotional development. Some worry that children will become so accustomed to all the attention that it will become difficult for them to adjust to normal life once the cameras stop following them around. In 2013, Jon Gosselin of *Jon & Kate Plus 8*, a program following a couple who had a set of sextuplets as well as a set of twins, claimed that being on reality television for so much of their lives had affected the moral compasses of his children—that they had problems interacting with their peers and with talking to other people when they were not on camera. These critics claim that losing this attention could cause the children to act out in negative ways. Also, the fact that children on reality shows are not playing a character but simply being themselves can make it more difficult and personal when people who watch the show post mean things on entertainment websites, social media websites, or blogs about the children.

Others are disturbed by the pressure on children featured in shows such as *Dance Moms* and *Toddlers and Tiaras*. They believe that the parents, eager for fame and fortune, sometimes ignore the needs of their children. Television critic Andy Denhart agreed with these criticisms but argued that good can come from these shows too. He said, "There's certainly a lot of social value

Taking Shows with a Grain of Salt

Some shows are not exploitative or charged with negative emotions, but if viewers do not keep in mind that they are watching a manipulated version of reality, they may encounter problems. In an article for the *Huffington Post*, journalist Geoff Williams wrote, "You probably wouldn't watch 'The Big Bang Theory' to help you land a job as a physicist or watch an episode of 'Game of Thrones' instead of studying for a medieval history test."[1] In contrast, real estate agents say there is an "HGTV effect" on people buying homes, in which people who watch a lot of home improvement shows tend to believe they are real estate experts. This can lead to confusion, mistakes, and disappointment. For example, on shows such as *House Hunters*, the buyers typically find a home they love after looking at only three houses. However, the footage on these shows is cut down to fit into a half-hour program. In reality, many people search dozens of houses for one that meets most of their requirements, and it frequently takes people more than a year to find the right one.

Other issues can arise as well. Elizabeth Ann Stribling-Kilvan, president of a New York City real estate agency, said, "While these home improvement shows are entertaining, they create this idea that properties need to be *perfect* in order to sell."[2] She and other agents agreed that people tend to look too closely at superficial things that could easily be replaced, such as outdated appliances or old countertops. This can lead them to pick a home that looks nice but has a lot of structural problems, which are harder and more expensive to fix. Real estate experts say there is no harm in watching a renovation or house hunting show and picking up a few tips along the way—as long as viewers keep in mind that, as with all reality shows, they are not seeing the whole truth.

1. Geoff Williams, "Bad Real Estate Lessons You've Learned from Watching HGTV," *Huffington Post*, October 9, 2018. www.huffpost.com/entry/bad-real-estate-lessons-hgtv_n_5bbb74d9e4b028e1fe 3fd014.
2. Quoted in Williams, "Bad Real Estate Lessons."

in illustrating the insane pressure adults place on kids while convincing themselves that it is for the kids' own good. TLC, Lifetime, and reality television producers did not create or cause this, and there's a possibility that broadcasting it could help stop it."[40]

Exploitation and Reality TV

Children are not the only ones whose exploitation people are concerned about. Many also question whether the potential damage to participants in shows that focus on people with mental and emotional disorders, such as *Hoarders*, outweighs the financial benefits to sponsors. Shows such as *Celebrity Rehab* and *Intervention*, which feature participants with substance abuse problems, have also been criticized. Programs such as these have become very popular in the last few years due to the public's fascination with dysfunctional lifestyles, but they tend to be more voyeuristic than other types of shows. As Julia Bricklin of *Forbes* magazine put it, "We are … concerned with whether mom will finish off her bottle of mouthwash in order to maintain her alcoholic haze … We want to know how grandma has managed to use diapers as her toilet for five years, and live with the stench, or how a trove of dogs and cats can die under a mountain of Campbell soup cans and uncle doesn't care."[41]

Hoarders, *My Strange Addiction*, and similar shows focus on people with mental health issues. Critics say these shows exploit the participants of the show by exposing to public ridicule a very real, private struggle that impacts the person's life and the lives of their loved ones. Supporters claim the purpose of these programs is to enable people to get help, which is admirable, but many others argue that their true purpose is to allow fascinated viewers to watch people living lives that are completely foreign to their own. There are other criticisms too. While the shows offer immediate help by bringing in experts such as cleanup crews and psychologists, critics say this approach can be too intense and overwhelming for the person to handle. Much like criticisms against weight-loss competition shows, experts argue that things need to be done gently and slowly, taking one step at a time, in order to create lasting change. People sometimes become depressed after the camera crews leave and the interest they felt in changing their habits disappears. In response to these criticisms, *Hoarders* implemented support systems, such as therapy and organizing help, that participants can access even after the show ends. Supporters of the show applaud this as well as the idea of exposing a problem that is often hidden. They feel that viewing the show might inspire others who are quietly struggling to recognize that they have a problem and seek help.

Physical Danger and Emotional Damage

The practice of encouraging people with mental illnesses to participate in reality programs such as Hoarders *has often been called exploitative.*

Although producers try their best to keep reality show participants safe, sometimes problems arise. On several occasions, cast members have participated on reality shows despite having been in trouble with the law for physical fights—an indication that they have quick tempers and might potentially put their fellow cast members at risk. For example, on the second season of *Big Brother*, Justin Sebik held a knife to the throat of another Houseguest. It was later discovered that Sebik had been arrested three times for assault, but the charges had been dismissed. In 2003, police raided the house used by *The Real World: San Diego* while the show was filming to investigate a report that a woman was raped in the bathroom by a friend of one of the participants.

Of course, people with criminal backgrounds also work on scripted shows. However, participants on reality shows generally work with fewer legal protections since the contracts they sign state outright that the producers are not responsible for bad things that may happen during filming. Additionally, producers of reality shows are looking for people with over-the-top personalities and in their search, sometimes fail to do their due diligence in background checks. For instance, in 2018, a *Bachelorette* contestant named Lincoln Adim was found guilty for a sexual assault he committed in 2016. The producers claimed Adim had been allowed on the show because the results of his background check had not included the incident or any other relating to sexual misconduct. This desire to cast volatile personalities, combined with the fact that producers are often actively attempting to create conflict for ratings and storytelling purposes, can lead to obvious consequences.

More common than physical danger, though, is emotional and mental damage. Many shows involve people being criticized on-camera, sometimes in very harsh ways. For instance, celebrity chef Gordon Ramsay has become famous for his insults and criticisms on reality TV shows such as *Hell's Kitchen* and *MasterChef*. While the insults are sometimes witty and humorous, making them fun to watch, the people who are participating on the show often feel very hurt by them. Their emotional turmoil is increased by the fact that they are in a televised competition—a tense situation they are not used to being in. It can be increased even further if the person has diagnosed or undiagnosed psychological issues, such as depression, bipolar disorder, or post-traumatic stress disorder (PTSD).

In 2018, Jessie Glenn, who had been a contestant on the third season of *MasterChef*, gave several interviews about her experience. She is one of the only people who is legally able to speak about everything that happens behind the scenes of reality shows because *MasterChef*'s lawyers somehow overlooked the fact that she had never signed the contract forbidding her to discuss it. Glenn explained that every step of the process was designed to put the maximum amount of stress on the participants. Some of the participants are recruited because they are odd and will make for good TV; Glenn's season included a chef with puppets and a self-proclaimed witch who tried to put a spell on the judges, but she said they were recruited "for comic relief rather than a quick advance to the finals."[42] It was their personalities, not their cooking, that got them on the show.

For the regular contestants such as Glenn, the tryout process was more stressful. She described having to meet with a psychiatrist and take a two-hour personality test. She believed "the point of the test is to judge what dramatic traits each person has that could be harvested later for a plot twist ... More generally, the test was an attempt to predict behavior in various situations. Or, what TV producers would call plotlines."[43] In other words, the tests, according to Glenn, were helping the producers script the show by predicting what would be the most dramatic. Glenn also had to speak to a detective about any potentially embarrassing or illegal situations she might have been part of in the past and was required to submit blood and urine samples for testing. The contract she did not sign

> asked me to agree to be subjected to physical and mental distress, to agree to have my medical history used in any way that they wanted ... to agree that my family would likely not be contacted in the case of an emergency ... They asked that I release them from liability from the social and economic losses that could result and to please note that the consequences could be substantial and could permanently change the future for me, my family, friends, and significant others.[44]

Glenn explained that once on set, everything seemed deliberately planned to put the contestants under as much stress as possible—yet the producers and other crew members persisted in telling the cast that nothing was prearranged or scripted. For instance, the contestant minders, who were referred to as "wranglers,"

> made a huge deal out of telling us our roommate selections were random ... [but] that appeared impossible. Everything the wranglers said seemed a pretty obvious setup to me to add intensity and create plotlines ... They had asked me about religion; Atheist, I said. And food: all local and organic! So I was roomed with a devout Evangelical Christian woman who used sugar, Rice Krispies and food coloring to make statues of the judges' heads, which she brought with her from Texas.[45]

This type of deliberate unsettling of the competitors continued throughout filming in various ways. Glenn had thought she was immune to most of it because she did not care as much about winning as she did about having the experience, but when she returned home, she "was a little screwed up ... Anxious, neurotic, easily startled and sobbing off and on for the next week ... I learned later from speaking with a number of runner-up cooks that every round longer that a contestant stayed in the competition, the symptoms of traumatic stress appeared more intense when they returned home."[46] The runner-up on Glenn's season, a man named Joshua Marks, was diagnosed with bipolar disorder and schizophrenia after the show ended that appeared to have been worsened by his time on the show—for example, in an episode of psychosis, he claimed to have been possessed by Gordon Ramsay. Marks killed himself a year after he appeared on *MasterChef*.

Contestants on other shows have exhibited similar mental problems and attempted or completed suicide as well. One of the most publicized involved Susan Boyle, who was briefly hospitalized for a mental breakdown after she appeared on *Britain's Got Talent*. Several months before that, a woman named Paula Goodspeed had committed suicide after being insulted by judge Simon Cowell. An investigation into the issue in 2009 found that at least 11 former reality show participants had killed themselves, but experts say that the real number is certainly higher. According to the British newspaper the *Independent*, "So widespread is the problem that some US psychiatrists now specialise in preventing former reality TV stars from taking their own life."[47] Mental health professionals have criticized reality TV producers for taking advantage of people who are vulnerable by not doing an effective job of screening their applicants for mental health issues and not taking care of the participants during and after filming.

Young Viewers and Reality TV

So what does all this mean for young viewers of reality television? Are these programs—and all the debates and scandals surrounding them—harmful to children and teens, or are reality shows just harmless entertainment? As with most other broad societal concerns, opinions are decidedly mixed.

Some sources believe that much of reality programming is a bad influence on today's youth. The Parents Television Council (PTC), a U.S.-based censorship advocacy group, has completed several studies on reality TV as a genre and has concerns about its effects on children.

A 2011 study by the PTC focused on four of the most popular reality programs on MTV at the time (*Jersey Shore*, *Teen Mom*, *16 and Pregnant*, and *The Real World*) and how they portrayed the behavior of men and women. The council was concerned that these shows were influencing the social development of young girls and boys. The study found that only 24 percent of what women on these shows said about themselves was positive and that women said more negative things than men when talking about themselves or other women. It also found that of the many references to sex made on the programs, only 3.6 percent of them involved virginity, contraception, or sexually transmitted diseases. The PTC concluded, "There remains an overwhelming message to young girls that their only unique and valued quality is their sexuality. The message to males is that they should lack [outward] emotion, be uninterested in relationships, and be defined by sexual conquests."[48]

However, even the PTC admits that some educational reality shows are worthwhile, and others believe that reality show critics underestimate today's youth and their ability to tell fact from fiction and right from wrong. Louisa Stein, professor of Film and Media Culture at Middlebury College, said that she believes young people today often watch reality programs to criticize them and make fun of them, rather than to imitate the behavior on them. "Hate-watching" as a pastime has exploded in recent years, especially with the increasing use of social media websites such as Facebook and Twitter, where people can broadcast their observations to millions of people at once. As journalist Margaret Bernstein stated, "Raised on a steady diet of reality TV, YouTube and Facebook, young people today are exceptionally media literate, and are quite used to observing, rating and critiquing the personal stories they see spilling across their television screens and computer monitors."[49]

However, this is only true insofar as the viewers remember that what they are seeing is not truly real. This can be difficult even for adults to remember because of how skilled most TV editors are and how well the producers manipulate the events and participants. Another 2011 study, this one released by the Girl Scouts of America, found that more than half the girls surveyed "believed what they were seeing [on reality shows] was 'mainly real and unscripted' … [and that] girls who were regular consumers of reality television were much more likely to believe that gossiping was a normal part of female friendships than their counterparts who didn't watch reality television."[50] The survey also upheld past research showing that regular viewing of reality TV increases relational aggression in real life.

Experts agree that parents should monitor what their children are watching and make an effort to watch programs with them to help them develop critical thinking skills and question what they are being shown. Anything can be educational if it is viewed in the proper context, and anything can be harmful if viewed in the wrong context. This means that there is no definitive answer on whether reality TV is harmful: for some it may be, while for others it may not. The key factor appears to be how willing the viewer is to believe that what they are watching has not been manipulated.

CHAPTER 5

Reality Television in the Future

When it first exploded into the public consciousness in the early 2000s, reality programming was considered by some to be a passing fad that would not last very long, and this might have been the case if not for a crucial event: the 2007 Writers Guild of America strike. Nearly every writer in Hollywood went on a three-month-long strike over a contract dispute, leading panicked television executives to green-light dozens of new reality programs to fill the prime time hours. As Americans waited for their favorite scripted programs to resume production, they got hooked on reality TV shows such as *The Apprentice* and *Keeping Up with the Kardashians*. Even after the scripted shows came back on the air, reality TV stayed at the top of the ratings.

More than a decade later, the genre is still going strong; it even has its own categories at the Emmy Awards. College courses on reality television are now offered at schools such as Indiana University and San Jose State University. Many forms of media reference reality programming on an increasingly common basis, even in articles that have nothing to do with television. For example, in an article about the presidential debate between Barack Obama and Mitt Romney held on October 3, 2012, columnist Gail Collins mused on whether or not undecided viewers had tuned into the debate by saying, "Maybe they [did], under the impression that it's another reality show about pawnbrokers, except this time they wear really nice suits."[51]

The Influence of Reality TV

Reality shows have had a notable influence on other forms of entertainment. The genre's influence on its scripted television counterparts is often obvious. Scripted programs such as *The Office*, *Modern Family*, and *Parks and Recreation* have been filmed documentary-style (also called mockumentary) and have made use of "confessional" interviews with characters who speak directly to the camera. These are not unlike interviews with participants on reality shows such as *The Bachelor*, *Survivor*, and *The Real World*.

Other scripted television shows have been developed in an attempt to cash in on the popularity of a particular reality program. Sources report that the hugely successful show *Lost* came about because ABC asked show creator J.J. Abrams to come up with a scripted version of *Survivor*. *Glee*, which featured pop songs sung by its characters, owed much to the appeal of *American Idol*. (*Glee*, in turn, spawned its own reality program, *The Glee Project*, in which contestants competed for a chance to appear on the scripted show.)

Shown here are people waiting in line to audition for The Glee Project.

As for the big screen, fictional stories presented as reality are found there too. A classic example is *The Blair Witch Project*, which was released in 1999. The film follows three students who travel into the woods of Maryland to film a documentary about a local legend called the Blair Witch. The students disappear in the woods, and *The Blair Witch Project* is supposedly the footage filmed by the three students that was recovered after they disappeared. This type of "found footage" movie is common today, but at the time, it was groundbreaking and new. A clever marketing campaign even convinced some people that the movie was real.

In addition, moviegoers have become more familiar with the concept of mixing reality and storytelling, which has resulted in an increase in films based on true stories. As Steven Zeitchik wrote in the *Los Angeles Times*, "Experts say that after a decade of reality television, the film business is finally catching up. Audiences and studio executives now not only tolerate a dose of real life in their feature films, they expect it. Stories … go from ordinary to powerful in the minds of filmgoers the moment 'based on a true story' flashes across the screen."[52] Some examples of such films from the last few decades include *127 Hours*, *The Social Network*, *Green Book*, *Argo*, and *Bohemian Rhapsody*.

Even the world of publishing has been affected by reality television, with concepts from reality programming appearing in the storylines of books. Perhaps the best-known example of this is the wildly popular book and movie series *The Hunger Games*, which centers on a fight-to-the-death competition among children that is televised live. Just as with real-life reality shows, the competitors in the game must deal with the show's producers manipulating the events and environment around them to maximize the drama. *The Hunger Games* is not the first example in the genre, however. Stephen King's novel *The Running Man*, published in 1982—after *An American Family* aired but before reality TV became widespread—focuses on a dystopian future in which the television landscape is ruled by brutal, violent, and frequently fatal game shows.

The Hunger Games *not only has an interesting plot, it also offers social commentary on reality shows and class divisions.*

The Internet and Reality TV

For years, the internet has served as an influence, companion, and additional source of reality programming. The "fly-on-the-wall" concept of watching things happen in real time has been present on the World Wide Web for many years. The first live image to be shown on the internet via webcam was a coffeepot in the Trojan Room at England's Cambridge University. A team of scientists set up the webcam in 1993 to check whether or not there was any coffee in the pot before they left their offices and headed down several flights of stairs to the Trojan Room. The site was live until 2001, by which time it had attracted 2.4 million visitors, despite showing nothing more thrilling than the coffeepot slowly filling and being emptied. According to Dan Gordon, one of the scientists, "Once, some American tourists called into the tourist information center here and asked where (the coffee pot) was so they could visit it … They took lots of photos."[53]

It was not long before webcam broadcasts began to feature human subjects, and now people can potentially make millions of dollars per year by making their own videos and broadcasting

The Truman Show

The Truman Show is a fictional movie starring Jim Carrey that premiered in 1998. In it, Carrey plays Truman, the first human in history to be televised live 24 hours a day for his entire life. The producers of the show have created an entire fake world for Truman to live in and manipulated all the events around him to create a compelling plotline for viewers. Truman has no idea until unexplainable things start happening to him.

Since the movie's release, people have occasionally speculated that one day a real-life version of *The Truman Show* might be created. Some believe it is inevitable, considering how popular reality shows are. Others say that if it were real, no one would watch. As journalist Dustin Grinnell noted, "it'd be deadly boring. We'd turn on the TV and see our man brushing his teeth. Paying bills. Flipping through magazines. Sleeping … It'd be too far. We wouldn't pity Truman, we'd pity ourselves for delighting in such profound meddling."[1]

The formerly outlandish premise of The Truman Show, *in which a man has every moment of his life unwittingly broadcast on television, no longer seems so far-fetched to some people.*

1. Dustin Grinnell, "We Know Reality TV Is Fake, So Why Do We Treat It Like It's Real?," *Thought Catalog*, November 2, 2017, thoughtcatalog.com/dustin-grinnell/2017/11/we-know-reality-tv-is-fake-so-why-do-we-treat-it-like-its-real/.

them on YouTube and other streaming websites. Some, such as Jenna Marbles (Jenna Nicole Mourey), Tyler Oakley, the Try Guys, and the Dolan Twins are known primarily through their work on these websites. Others have used their rise to fame on YouTube to work on new projects. For example, Justin Bieber became famous after uploading videos of himself singing, and Bethany Mota, a beauty and fashion blogger, participated in season 19 of *Dancing with the Stars*. Still others are famous for multiple reasons. For example, John Green, author of *The Fault in Our Stars*, published his first novel, *Looking for Alaska*, in 2005. In 2007, he and his brother Hank started a popular YouTube channel called Vlogbrothers, which they continued to run even as John published more best-selling books.

In 2011, the website YouNow was launched, with its creators claiming that it was the first online reality network. It is a social entertainment platform where users upload live video of themselves and receive feedback on the content from the website's audience in real time.

Social Media and Reality TV

Social media outlets, such as Facebook, Twitter, and Instagram, and message boards on websites also link together reality TV and the internet. Producer Mark Burnett has credited the success of some shows to social media. It is very common for people to "live-tweet" television programs as they happen, and some particularly popular television events collect hundreds of thousands of tweets from start to end. Many shows have forums dedicated specifically to them, where people can discuss the episodes each week. For instance, on *Amazing Race* forums, fans discuss their opinions of the contestants, who they think will be eliminated, and how they felt about the challenges and eliminations.

In 2012, the *Hollywood Reporter* conducted a poll on social media and the impact of Facebook and Twitter on entertainment users. The poll revealed the strong effect of social media on television: Three out of ten people responded that they watched a television show because of something they saw on a social media website. Of the respondents, 76 percent said they posted about shows while watching them live, 41 percent reported tweeting about the show they were watching, and 46 percent stated that reality programs were the ones about which they were most likely to post comments online.

REALITY SHOWS AFFECT REAL LIFE

"Hyped-up tension on television cookery shows is leading to a nationwide chef shortage, industry figures have warned. ... Shows such as MasterChef and The Great British Bake Off (GBBO) have ... made one in five [British people] question their own culinary skills, feeling they are not good enough and so would not even consider working in a kitchen."

–Victoria Ward, British journalist

Victoria Ward, "Hyped-Up Tension on TV Cookery Shows Leading to Chef Shortages, Figures Warn," Telegraph, November 27, 2018. www.telegraph.co.uk/news/2018/11/27/hyped-up-tension-tv-cookery-shows-leading-chef-shortage-figures/.

Some reality competitions allow viewers to cast votes through social media outlets. In 2011, *The X Factor* became the first show to offer fans the option to vote through Twitter, and *The Voice* and *American Idol* soon followed suit. Later, all three shows developed apps specific to the show. Although people can still vote in other ways without downloading the apps, they include features that are meant to enhance the viewing experience, such as polls and quizzes. *The Voice*'s app even lets viewers suggest songs they want the artists to perform. Social media voting methods concern some fans, however. One forum poster responded to the news about *The Voice*'s social media presence by stating,

> In terms of using social media to vote, I'd find it much sketchier if [The Voice] allowed voting through Twitter (through use of a hash tag or something along those lines ...) I fear the power voting could get out of control if someone with a ton of followers like [Justin] Bieber or Kim Kardashian started urging their fans to retweet a hash-tagged vote for one contestant.[54]

This comment was posted partly in response to an incident during *The Voice*'s first season, when Justin Bieber encouraged his Twitter followers to vote for Javier Colon. Colon won the competition, and some claimed the victory was an outcome of Bieber's influence rather than Colon's personal popularity.

Facebook fan pages and online forums have become very popular with viewers, and producers pay attention to this. They sometimes assign staff members to read the posts and Twitter feeds and see what the fans are saying so they can adjust the television shows accordingly. This makes social media similar to a free, widespread, diverse focus group that allows the producers to see viewers' reactions in real time. Producers also sometimes work with cast members to create social media profiles that provide viewers with more personal information about the cast members, and some shows require stars to maintain and update personal social media accounts. The producers of *American Idol* even managed to find a way to profit from Facebook. In 2011, they offered users the chance to send video messages from the contestants to other Facebook

Producers sometimes work with reality show cast members to create and update Facebook profiles and Twitter accounts for fan interaction.

users for $1. Today, people are more likely to simply tweet at their favorite celebrities. Social media engagement with one's fans is an important factor in today's celebrity culture. It makes a celebrity seem relatable and connected to their fan base. Nearly everyone is on some form of social media; it is one of the single most influential platforms in American society today. Simon Cowell once dismissed the effect of Twitter on his shows but has since changed his mind, stating, "The only powerful people now on TV are the people on Twitter and Facebook."[55]

What Comes Next?

It seems likely that reality TV will continue well into the foreseeable future. According to Herb Terry, who developed the course on reality TV at Indiana University, "We've been saying for years that the future of television would no longer be as a stand-alone medium, that it would be a medium that would somehow interact with everything else. Reality TV may be the best example running right now."[56] Indeed, because many of its programs depend on audience interaction and engagement, reality TV seems far ahead of scripted programming in this respect. It is easy for people to feel passionate about a program they feel they have an investment in, whether they are voting for their favorite contestants on a competition program or hate-tweeting their way through the season finale of *Real Housewives of New Jersey*.

The cost factor is another reason why reality programming will likely remain around indefinitely: It is much cheaper to produce a reality show than it is to produce a scripted one. Sources in the entertainment business claim that it costs between $700,000 and $1.6 million to produce an hour of reality television, while it costs $2 million to $3 million to produce an hour of scripted programming. One reason for this cost savings is that reality show cast members earn less than actors on scripted programs. Producers also save money because the writers on reality shows are not covered by Writers Guild of America (WGA) contracts. As a result, the writers have no guaranteed wages or standard benefits such as health insurance. This has been a major source of debate in the tele-vision industry, because the WGA believes this is not fair to the writers.

An Unhealthy Obsession with Fame

Many people dream of being the star of their own reality program. For most, dreaming is as far as it goes. However, some hopefuls have gone to great–and illegal–lengths to attract attention.

In 2009, Richard and Mayumi Heene, a couple who had formerly appeared twice on *Wife Swap*, contacted police, tearfully claiming that a large helium balloon had taken off with their six-year-old son inside. A massive rescue effort was launched, and it seemed the entire world was watching in horror as the balloon drifted across the Colorado skies. When the balloon finally landed, however, the boy was not inside. He was later found hiding in the attic of his home. It turned out that the entire incident was a stunt created by the Heenes to generate publicity in hopes of landing their own reality show. Instead, the Heenes were fined and served jail time.

Also in 2009, Tareq and Michaele Salahi showed up uninvited to a dinner at the White House. The two were being considered as cast members for Bravo's show *The Real Housewives of D.C.* at the time and were filmed by a crew while preparing for the evening. When it was revealed that they were not actually on the guest list, the Salahis were investigated by a federal grand jury. In spite of the federal investigation, they managed to reach their goal and become part of the *Housewives* cast.

It is hard to predict exactly how reality programming will unfold in the near future, but the genre appears to be con-tinuing to explore a wide variety of topics and issues. Reality producers seem willing to try to make almost any subject inter-esting to the viewing public—for a profit. As long as people are willing to watch reality participants, producers will continue to put those shows on TV.

However, with the rise of streaming services such as Netflix and Hulu, the number of people watching cable TV is decreasing. For this reason, some production companies have partnered with these services so their shows can be broadcast to a wider audience. TV viewership is not the only thing waning, though. The popularity of reality shows in general has decreased noticeably in recent years, going from a driving force in television to barely cracking the top 10 most popular shows. The *New York Times* reported in November 2018 that viewership for once-popular shows has declined dramatically: "*Dancing with the Stars* has stumbled for ABC, down more than 31 percent this year. Add in a loss of 33 percent in the audience for ABC's *Shark Tank*, and you have a trend that is keeping producers of so-called unscripted television awake at night."[57]

It is unlikely that reality TV will ever disappear completely, but it seems that many viewers are growing tired of it. For this reason, many in the entertainment business believe the future will bring new twists and tweaks to the formats of reality programs. The longer reality TV is around, the more producers will have to tweak shows to make them different than what people have seen before and keep interest fresh. In a 2012 interview with the *Hollywood Reporter*, producer Jonathan Murray reflected on how reality television has had to evolve over the years. When asked if he thought *The Real World* would sell at MTV if he pitched it to them today, he said, "I'm not sure we could sell it today … Today you start with a *Real World* idea of either putting people in a house, then you have to add the additional elements—they're all bad girls, they're all from the *Jersey Shore*—to make it loud enough to capture people's attention."[58]

Two things remain certain. First, as long as reality television exists, people will continue to debate whether it is educational, entertaining, or harmful. Second, as long as it remains popular, producers will continue to put shows on the air. People are constantly broadcasting their own lives to the world and hoping that somebody is interested enough to help them turn it into a career. According to television critic James Poniewozik,

> There are ... American ideas that reality TV taps into: That everybody should have a shot. That sometimes being real is better than being polite. That no matter where you started out, you can hit it big, get lucky and reinvent yourself ... And most important, that you can find something interesting in the lives of people other than celebrities, lawyers and doctors ... It is as if, as a society, we had been singing in front of a mirror for generations, only to discover that now the mirror can actually see us. And if we are really lucky, it might just offer us a show.[59]

Introduction: A Dominant Force in Television

1. Neil Genzlinger, "Have I Got a Show for You ..." *New York Times*, March 31, 2011. www.nytimes.com/2011/04/03/arts/television/reality-shows-can-you-guess-the-fakes.html?pagewanted=all.

2. James Poniewozik, "Why Reality TV Is Good for Us," *TIME*, February 12, 2003. www.time.com/time/magazine/article/0,9171,421047,00.html.

3. Quoted in Michael Ventre, "Will 2011 Be the Year Reality TV Dies?," *Today*, January 3, 2011. today.msnbc.msn.com/id/40753472/ns/today-entertainment/t/will-be-year-reality-tv-dies.

Chapter 1: Defining Reality Television

4. Quoted in Bethany Ogdon, "The Psycho-Economy of Reality Television in the 'Tabloid Decade,'" in *How Real Is Reality TV?: Essays on Representation and Truth*, ed. David S. Escoffery. Jefferson, NC: McFarland, 2006, pp. 29–30.

5. Robin Nabi, Erica Biely, Sara Morgan, and Carmen Stitt, "Reality-Based Television Programming and the Psychology of Its Appeal," *Media Psychology*, vol. 5, no. 4, 2003, p. 304.

6. Matthew Gilbert, "The House That Roared," *Boston Globe*, March 6, 2011. archive.boston.com/ae/tv/articles/2011/03/06/mtvs_the_real_world_has_influenced_a_generation_of_reality_shows/?page=1.

7. Andy Denhart, "25 Seasons On, Real World as Immature as Ever," *Today*, March 14, 2011. www.today.com/popculture/25-seasons-real-world-immature-ever-wb-na41987240.

8. Mark Andrejevic, *Reality TV: The Work of Being Watched.* Lanham, MD: Rowman & Littlefield, 2004, p. 72.

9. Quoted in Ashley Fantz, "Reality Shows Revolutionize Arab TV," CNN, March 17, 2012. www.cnn.com/2012/03/17/world/arab-reality-shows/index.html.

10. Lisa O'Carroll, "Arab Reality Show Jilted by Runaway Bride," *Guardian*, March 1, 2004. www.theguardian.com/media/2004/mar/01/race.broadcasting.

Chapter 2: Why Is Reality Television Popular?

11. Eric Jaffe, "Reality Check," *Observer*, vol. 18, no. 3, 2005. www.psychologicalscience.org/observer/reality-check.

12. Quoted in Jaffe, "Reality Check."

13. Christopher E. Bell, *American Idolatry: Celebrity, Commodity, and Reality Television.* Jefferson, NC: McFarland, 2010, p. 75.

14. Quoted in Jesse Hicks, "Probing Question: Why Do We Love Reality Television?," Penn State News, August 24, 2009. news.psu.edu/story/141303/2009/08/24/research/probing-question-why-do-we-love-reality-television.

15. Sydney Lipez, interview by Shannon Kelly, March 2012.

16. Quoted in Richard E. Crew, "How Real Is Survivor for Its Viewers?," in *How Real Is Reality TV?: Essays on Representation and Truth*, ed. David S. Escoffery. Jefferson, NC: McFarland, 2006, p. 71.

17. Robin Nabi, Carmen R. Stitt, Jeff Halford, and Keli L. Finnerty, "Emotional and Cognitive Predictors of the Enjoyment of Reality-Based and Fictional Television Programming: An Elaboration of the Uses and Gratifications Perspective," *Media Psychology*, vol. 8, no. 4, 2006, pp. 431–432.

Chapter 3: Start Getting "Real"

18. Quoted in Keith Hollihan, "The Omarosa Experiment," *Morning News*, January 17, 2006. www.themorningnews. org/article/the-omarosa-experiment.

19. Quoted in Dustin Grinnell, "We Know Reality TV Is Fake, so Why Do We Treat It Like It's Real?," *Thought Catalog*, November 2, 2017. thoughtcatalog.com/dustin-grinnell/2017/11/ we-know-reality-tv-is-fake-so-why-do-we-treat-it-like-its-real/.

20. Quoted in Jeff Greenfield, "The Real Deal on Reality TV," CBS News, February 7, 2010. www.cbsnews.com/2100-3445_162-6183037.html.

21. Anna Klassen, "I Was on Reality TV: Behind the Scenes Secrets of Faking Real Life," *Huffington Post*, December 6, 2017. www.huffingtonpost.com/bustle/i-was-on-reality-tv-faking-real-life_b_4823714.html.

22. Derek Woodruff, interview by Shannon Kelly, March 2012.

23. Quoted in Andrejevic, *Reality TV*, p. 104.

24. Quoted in Hollihan, "The Omarosa Experiment."

25. Quoted in Hollihan, "The Omarosa Experiment."

26. Quoted in Craig Thomashoff, "Casting Reality TV? It's Now Difficult to Find Real People," *New York Times*, August 25, 2011. www.nytimes.com/2011/08/28/arts/ television/casting-reality-tv-has-become-more-difficult. html.

27. Edward Wyatt, "TV Contestants: Tired, Tipsy and Pushed to Brink," *New York Times*, August 2, 2009. www.nytimes.com/2009/08/02/business/media/02reality. html?pagewanted=all.

28. Quoted in Carrie Brownstein, "*The Bachelor* and Other Delights," *Monitor Mix*, NPR, April 28, 2008. www.npr.org/ blogs/monitormix/2008/04/the_bachelor_1.html.

29. Grinnell, "We Know Reality TV Is Fake."

30. Quoted in Kim Reed, "It's Time to Stop Blaming the Editing," *Today*, November 29, 2004. today.msnbc.msn.com/id/6407884/ns/today-entertainment/t/its-time-stop-blaming-editing.

31. Anonymous, interview by Anna North, "Career Confidential: A Reality TV Editor Reveals the Most and Least Fake Shows," BuzzFeed, August 22, 2012. www.buzzfeed.com/buzzfeedshift/career-confidential-a-reality-tv-editor-reveals-t.

32. "So You Think You Can Dance 2018 Voting Frequently Asked Questions," Fox, accessed on December 3, 2018. www.fox.com/so-you-think-you-can-dance/article/so-you-think-you-can-dance-2018-voting-frequently-asked-questions-5b5b966265ee56001bab793a/.

33. Quoted in Joal Ryan, "No 'Idol' Controversy," *E! Online*, August 20, 2002. www.eonline.com/news/No__quot_Idol_quot__Controversy/43755.

Chapter 4: Positives and Negatives

34. James Poniewozik, "Television: Why Reality TV Is Good for Us," *TIME*, February 17, 2003. www.time.com/time/magazine/article/0,9171,1004251-1,00.html.

35. "Viewer Beware: Watching Reality TV Can Impact Real-Life Behavior," *All Things Considered*, NPR, August 24, 2014. www.npr.org/2014/08/24/342429563/viewer-beware-watching-reality-tv-can-impact-real-life-behavior.

36. Quoted in Andrea Canning and Elizabeth Stuart, "Reality Show Violence Getting Too Real?," ABC News, March 30, 2011. abcnews.go.com/Entertainment/reality-tv-show-violence-real-life-consequences-teen/story?id=13256971.

37. Quoted in Liane Bonin Starr, "Do You Have to Be Crazy to Be a Reality TV Star?," *HitFix*, UPROXX, September 1, 2011.

uproxx.com/hitfix/do-you-have-to-be-crazy-to-be-a-reality-tv-star/.

38. Allison Samuels, "Reality TV Trashes Black Women," *Newsweek*, May 1, 2011. www.newsweek.com/reality-tv-trashes-black-women-67641.

39. Quoted in Greg Braxton, "*The Bachelor, The Bachelorette* Creator Defends All-White Cast of Title Role," *Los Angeles Times*, March 18, 2011. articles.latimes.com/2011/mar/18/entertainment/la-et-bachelor-race-20110318.

40. Andy Denhart, "'Dance Moms,' 'Toddlers & Tiaras,' and Child Abuse," *Daily Beast*, January 25, 2012. www.thedailybeast.com/dance-moms-toddlers-and-tiaras-and-child-abuse.

41. Julia Bricklin, "Monday Night Rehab: A&E's 'Intervention' and 'Hoarders' Return," *Forbes*, January 3, 2012. www.forbes.com/sites/juliabricklin/2012/01/03/monday-night-rehab-aes-intervention-and-hoarders-return.

42. Jessie Glenn, "I Am a 'MasterChef' Survivor," *Salon*, February 18, 2018. www.salon.com/2018/02/17/i-am-a-master-chef-survivor/.

43. Glenn, "I Am a 'MasterChef' Survivor."

44. Glenn, "I Am a 'MasterChef' Survivor."

45. Glenn, "I Am a 'MasterChef' Survivor."

46. Glenn, "I Am a 'MasterChef' Survivor."

47. Guy Adams, "Lessons from America on the Dangers of Reality Television," *Independent*, June 6, 2009. www.independent.co.uk/news/world/americas/lessons-from-america-on-the-dangers-of-reality-television-1698165.html.

48. "Reality on MTV: Gender Portrayals on MTV Reality Programming," Parents Television Council, 2011. www.parentstv.org/PTC/publications/reports/MTV-RealityStudy/MTVRealityStudy_Dec11.pdf.

49. Michael Norman, "Does Reality TV for Teens Induce Bad Behavior?," Cleveland.com, March 15, 2008. www.cleveland.com/tv/index.ssf/2008/03/does_reality_tv_for_teens_indu.html.

50. Leah Campbell, "Reality TV Can be Unhealthy for Participants as Well as Viewers," Healthline, March 14, 2018. www.healthline.com/health-news/reality-tv-unhealthy-for-participants-and-viewers#1.

Chapter 5: Reality Television in the Future

51. Gail Collins, "Bobbing Along on a Sea of Debate Coverage," *Salt Lake Tribune*, October 4, 2012. archive.sltrib.com/article.php?id=55025308&itype=CMSID.

52. Steven Zeitchik, "From Real to Reel: In Fact-Based Films, Reality and Storytelling Collide," *Los Angeles Times*, December 27, 2010. articles.latimes.com/2010/dec/27/entertainment/la-et-movie-reality-20101227.

53. Quoted in "Farewell, Seminal Coffee Cam," *Wired*, March 7, 2001. www.wired.com/2001/03/farewell-seminal-coffee-cam/.

54. KerleyQ, Television Without Pity, March 31, 2012. forums.televisionwithoutpity.com/index.php?showtopic=3203407&st=4860.

55. Quoted in Brian Stelter, "Twitter and TV Get Close to Help Each Other Grow," *New York Times*, October 25, 2011. www.nytimes.com/2011/10/26/business/media/twitter-and-tv-get-close-to-help-each-other-grow.html.

56. Quoted in "Reality Television Not Just Fun Viewing for IU Students, but also a Serious College Course," IU News Room, October 13, 2003. newsinfo.iu.edu/news/page/normal/1148.html.

57. John Koblin, "The New TV Season: Reboots and Reality Shows Are Sinking. Fallon Counters a Move by Colbert," *New York Times*, November 25, 2018.

www.nytimes.com/2018/11/25/business/media/broadcast-networks-television-ratings.html.

58. Quoted in Lacey Rose and Stacey Wilson Hunt, "Bunim/Murray at 25," *Hollywood Reporter*, March 27, 2012. www.hollywoodreporter.com/news/bunim-murray-at-25-305542.

59. James Poniewozik, "Reality TV at 10: How It's Changed Television—and Us," *TIME*, February 22, 2010. www.time.com/time/magazine/article/0,9171,1963739-4,00.html.

Chapter 1: Defining Reality Television

1. Do you agree with the given definition of "reality television"?

2. Which shows, aside from those mentioned by the author, do not seem to fit neatly into any of the categories listed in the first chapter? Would you create any new categories?

3. In what ways do reality television shows in other parts of the world differ from those in the United States?

Chapter 2: Why Is Reality Television Popular?

1. Do you like to watch reality shows? Why or why not?

2. Do you agree with Nabi that most people do not watch reality TV for voyeuristic reasons?

3. Why do you think some people believe that reality TV fans are less intelligent than fans of scripted shows?

Chapter 3: Start Getting "Real"

1. Aside from "bad boy" and "party girl," what are some other stereotypical character types frequently seen on reality programs?

2. Why are some stereotypes on reality television seen as being harmful?

3. Watch an episode of a reality show. Can you identify points where the editing may have made a difference in how you felt about what you were watching?

Chapter 4: Positives and Negatives

1. Do you think watching violence or aggression on reality programs makes a person more likely to act that way in real life? Why or why not?

2. Why do you think it took so many years for *The Bachelorette* to cast a black lead?

3. Have you ever wanted to be on a reality show? Do you feel differently after reading this chapter?

Chapter 5: Reality Television in the Future

1. Why do you think people enjoy interacting on social media about the shows they watch?

2. Why is it so important for reality TV stars to have a strong social media presence?

3. How do you predict reality television will look 10 years from now?

ORGANIZATIONS TO CONTACT

American Psychological Association
750 First Street NE
Washington, DC 20002
(800) 374-2721
www.apa.org
> This association studies many aspects of the effects of television (including reality television) on people's behavior.

Common Sense Media
650 Townsend Street, Suite 435
San Francisco, CA 94103
(415) 863-0600
www.commonsensemedia.org
> This organization makes age-appropriate media recommendations for children. It also seeks to help kids become smart, responsible interpreters of television shows and other media.

Parents Television Council
707 Wilshire Boulevard, Ste. 2075
Los Angeles, CA 90017
(800) 882-6868
www.parentstv.org
> This organization monitors prime time television programs and helps parents decide whether or not a show is appropriate for children to watch.

FOR MORE INFORMATION

Books

DeVolld, Troy. *Reality TV: An Insider's Guide to TV's Hottest Market.* Studio City, CA: Michael Wiese, 2011.
> The author, who has worked in the TV industry, gives an overview of the history and types of reality programs and discusses how a reality show is produced.

Essany, Michael. *Reality Check: The Business and Art of Producing Reality TV.* Burlington, MA: Focal, 2008.
> This book explains the creation of reality television programming.

Otfinoski, Steven. *Television: From Concept to Consumer.* New York, NY: Children's Press, 2015.
> This book discusses multiple genres of TV shows, including reality shows, and how the ways they are made and advertised differ from each other.

Weil, Jamie. *Asking Questions About What's on Television.* Ann Arbor, MI: Cherry Lake Publishing, 2016.
> Some reality shows have positive messages, while others have negative ones. Learning to examine the behavior shown on TV and analyze the messages it sends is an important skill, which is discussed in this book.

Websites

Biography: Reality TV Stars
www.biography.com
> Searching "reality TV" on this website yields many news articles and biographies about former and current reality stars.

***Huffington Post*: Reality TV**
www.huffingtonpost.com/topic/reality-tv
> This section of the *Huffington Post*'s website contains articles on the latest reality TV news as well as opinion pieces about various aspects of the genre.

Reality Blurred
www.realityblurred.com
> This website features articles that review and analyze reality shows.

Reality TV World
www.realitytvworld.com
> This website features current news articles about a variety of reality shows.

INDEX

A

ABC, 18, 22, 48, 50, 55, 75, 84
Abdul, Paula, 54
Adim, Lincoln, 69
African reality shows, 29
aggression, 44, 56–58, 61, 73
Alaska State Troopers, 9
alcohol, 48, 57, 67
Amazing Race, The, 6, 8, 14, 23–24
American Family, An, 13, 17–20, 63, 76
American Idol, 25–26, 28, 34–35, 42, 54–55, 75, 80–81
American Idolatry (Bell), 33
American Ninja Warrior, 16
America's Most Wanted, 20
America's Next Top Model, 15, 25, 64
Apprentice, The, 25, 44–45, 47, 74
Arab reality shows, 28
Ashlee+Evan, 32–33
Australian reality shows, 23, 26

B

Bachelor, The, 6, 15, 24, 41, 45, 48–49, 61–63, 75
Bachelorette, The, 15, 25, 41, 63, 69
Bartsch, Jeff, 50
Beers, Thom, 47
Bell, Christopher E., 33
Bernstein, Margaret, 72
Bieber, Justin, 79–81
Big Brother, 12, 15, 23–26, 28–29, 46, 61–62, 68
Biggest Loser, The, 60–61
Blair Witch Project, The, 76
Blind Date, 50
body image, 58–59
Boggs, Kelly, 15
Bohemian Rhapsody, 35, 76
Born This Way, 9
Boyle, Susan, 71
Boy Meets Boy, 64
Bricklin, Julia, 67
British reality shows, 22, 25–26, 36, 80
Bunim, Mary-Ellis, 46–47
Burnett, Mark, 54, 79

C

cable, 7–8, 63, 84
"camp sensibility," 40
Candid Camera, 17–18
Carrey, Jim, 78
casting, 33, 43–45, 47, 63
Catfish: The TV Show, 13

children
    in reality shows, 18, 65, 76
    as viewers, 56, 71–73
Chinese reality shows, 27
Clarkson, Kelly, 34
Clinton, Bill, 22
Coelen, Chris, 44
Collins, Gail, 74
Communications Act of 1934,
    53
confidentiality agreements, 54
Cops, 20
Cowell, Simon, 34, 71, 82
Cronin, Mark, 51

D
Dance Moms, 65
Dancing with the Stars, 8,
    16–17, 25, 33–34, 55, 79,
    84
Dating Game, The, 50
Deadliest Catch, 47
Denhart, Andy, 21, 65
Destination Truth, 13
diversity, 43, 63, 81

E
Eisner, Michael, 58
Emmy Awards, 35, 74
Essany, Michael, 13, 15–16
exploitation, 15, 31, 66–68
Extreme Makeover franchise,
    15

F
Facebook, 47, 72, 79–82
Fear Factor, 16
First 48, The, 15, 61

"frankenbiting," 50
French reality shows, 26
Funt, Allen, 18

G
Galavis, Juan Pablo, 62
gender, 20, 25, 31, 43, 57,
    61, 64
German reality shows, 26
Gilbert, Craig, 19
Gilbert, Matthew, 20
Glenn, Jessie, 62, 69–71
Glynn, Kevin, 11
Goodspeed, Paula, 71
Goodstein, Anastasia, 64
Grinnell, Dustin, 49, 51, 78

H
Hatch, Richard, 45
HBO, 19
Hell's Kitchen, 48, 69
Hills, The, 48, 52
Hirschorn, Michael, 63
Hoarders, 13, 67–68
House Hunters, 66
Hunger Games, The (Collins),
    76–77

I
Impractical Jokers, 16
Indonesian reality shows, 28
Intervention, 51, 67

J
Japanese reality shows, 27
Jeopardy!, 6
Jersey Shore, 6, 38, 52, 56–57,
    72

Joe Millionaire, 9
Jon & Kate Plus 8, 65
Judge Judy, 11, 13

K
Kaiser, Stacey, 57
Kalil, Joe, 28
Kardashian West, Kim, 9–10, 80
Katzenberger, Daniela, 26
Keeping Up with the Kardashians, 13–14, 39, 74
Klassen, Anna, 45
Korean reality shows, 26–27

L
Lambert, Adam, 34–35
Latinx reality shows, 30
Levak, Richard, 44
LGBT+ community, 19–20, 22, 63–64
Limotte, Tabitha, 59
Lindsay, Rachel, 63
Little People, Big World, 9
Lost, 75
Loud, Lance, 18–19
Lythgoe, Nigel, 53

M
Macchio, Ralph, 33
Made, 16
Manigault Newman, Omarosa, 45
MasterChef, 26, 62, 69, 71, 80
mental health, 48, 65, 67–69, 71
Mercury, Freddie, 35
Million Dollar Listing, 6

Monroe, Courteney, 7
MTV, 7, 16–17, 20–22, 72
Murray, Jonathan, 47, 84
My 600-lb Life, 16

N
Nabi, Robin, 11–13, 38–39, 42
NBC, 17
Nicholson, Jenny, 36
Nicole, Jayde, 48

O
Opposite Worlds, 30, 36
Orloff, Judith, 58
Osbournes, The, 25

P
parasocial relationships, 42
Parents Television Council (PTC), 72
Parris, Megan, 45
Paul, Bryant, 32
Philbin, Matt, 34
plastic surgery, 14–15, 58–59
plotlines, 70, 78
Poniewozik, James, 8, 10, 23, 56, 85
Porter, Rick, 39
Price is Right, The, 6, 11
prime time, 7, 23
Project Runway, 9, 48, 64

Q
Queer Eye, 14, 61, 64

R
racial issues, 61–64

Ramsay, Gordon, 69, 71
Real Housewives franchise, 6, 9, 39, 49, 58, 61–62, 83
Reality Check: The Business and Art of Producing Reality TV (Essany), 13
Reality TV: The Work of Being Watched (Andrejevic), 23
Real People, 20
Real World, The, 7–8, 15, 17, 20–22, 46, 62, 64, 68, 72, 84
Rescue 911, 20
Revenge Body with Khloe Kardashian, 14, 59
Roberts, Burton, 46
Rock of Love with Bret Michaels, 16
Running Man, The (King), 76
RuPaul's Drag Race, 9, 64

S
safety, 36, 68
scripted shows, 7–8, 30–31, 48, 56, 58, 65, 74–75, 82
Sebik, Justin, 68
sexual assault, 56, 69
16 and Pregnant, 72
social media, 37, 65, 72, 79–82
Solovey, Sam, 47
So You Think You Can Dance, 14, 25, 35, 53
Stein, Louisa, 72
stereotypes, 40, 42–43, 61–63
Stillman, Stacey, 54
Storage Wars, 47
Storm Stories, 6

streaming services, 21, 79, 84
Stribling-Kilvan, Elizabeth Ann, 66
subgroups
    aspiration, 15
    celebrity, 13, 16–17, 25, 33
    competition, 14, 16–17, 21, 25, 29–30, 34, 45, 52–53, 57, 69, 80
    documentary, 13, 18, 26
    fear-based, 16
    forced environment, 15
    personal improvement and makeover, 14–15, 58–59
    professional, 15
    renovation and design, 15–16, 66
    romance, 15–16, 41–42, 62
    sports, 16
    undercover, 16–17
Sundar, S. Shyam, 35
Surreal Life, The, 14
Survivor, 8, 14, 23–26, 29, 31, 36, 38, 44–46, 54, 61, 75
Swan, The, 14–15

T
Teen Mom, 13, 72
Terry, Herb, 82
That's Incredible!, 20
TMZ on TV, 9
Toddlers and Tiaras, 65
Top Chef, 61
Total Bellas, 32
toxic masculinity, 61

Trading Spaces, 24
Trauma: Life in the ER, 6
Trojan Room coffeepot, 77
True Life, 13
Truman Show, The, 78
Trump, Donald, 9
Twitter, 37, 72, 79–82

U
Ultimate Fighter, 16
Uncle Jim's Question Bee, 17
Undercover Boss, 16
Underwood, Carrie, 35
Unsolved Mysteries, 20

V
Vanilla Ice Project, The, 16
Very Brady Renovation, A, 16
Very Cavallari, 32
View, The, 11
Voice, The, 6, 8, 12, 14,
    25–26, 35, 64, 80–81
voting, 14, 53–55, 80–81

voyeurism, 38–39, 41–42, 67

W
What Not to Wear, 14
White, Geoffrey, 37
Who Wants to Be a Millionaire?,
    22–23
Williams, Geoff, 66
Woodruff, Derek, 45
Writers Guild of America
    (WGA), 74, 82–83

X
X Factor, The, 80

Y
YouNow, 79
YouTube, 36, 72, 79

Z
Zamora, Pedro, 20, 22
Zeitchik, Steven, 76

ABOUT THE AUTHOR

Tyler Stevenson is a professional in the health insurance industry. He graduated from the University at Buffalo with a degree in sociology and originally went into banking before making the switch to health insurance. He works in Buffalo, New York, and lives in the City of Tonawanda with his wife, two young daughters, two dogs, two cats, and the family guinea pig, Pig-Pig.